KNOW YOUR GOVERNMENT

How the President Is Elected

The Constitution
The Democratic Party
The House of Representatives
How Laws Are Passed
How the President Is Elected
Impeachment
The Presidency
The Republican Party
The Senate
The Supreme Court

KNOW YOUR GOVERNMENT

How the President Is Elected

By Justine Rubinstein

MASON CREST
PHILADELPHIA • MIAMI

Mason Crest
450 Parkway Drive, Suite D
Broomall, Pennsylvania 19008
(866) MCP-BOOK (toll-free)
www.masoncrest.com

Copyright © 2020 by Mason Crest, an imprint of National Highlights, Inc. All rights reserved. No part of this publication may be reproduced or transmitted in any form or by any means, electronic or mechanical, including photocopying, recording, taping, or any information storage and retrieval system, without permission in writing from the publisher.

Printed in the United States of America
First printing
9 8 7 6 5 4 3 2 1

Series ISBN: 978-1-4222-4231-5
Hardcover ISBN: 978-1-4222-4236-0

Cataloging-in-Publication Data is available on file at the Library of Congress.

Developed and Produced by Print Matters Productions, Inc. (www.printmattersinc.com)
Cover and Interior Design by Lori S. Malkin Design, LLC

QR CODES AND LINKS TO THIRD-PARTY CONTENT:
You may gain access to certain third-party content ("third-party sites") by scanning and using the QR Codes that appear in this publication (the "QR Codes"). We do not operate or control in any respect any information, products or services on such third-party sites linked to by us via the QR Codes included in this publication, and we assume no responsibility for any materials you may access using the QR Codes. Your use of the QR Codes may be subject to terms, limitations, or restrictions set forth in the applicable terms of use or otherwise established by the owners of the third-party sites. Our linking to such third-party sites via the QR Codes does not imply an endorsement or sponsorship of such third-party sites, or the information, products, or services offered on or through the third-party sites, nor does it imply an endorsement or sponsorship of this publication by the owners of such third-party sites.

CONTENTS

INTRODUCTION: The Evolving American Experiment 6

Chapter 1 ★ Too Close to Call 10

Chapter 2 ★ Electing a President 20

Chapter 3 ★ The Electoral College 32

Chapter 4 ★ Party Politics 44

Chapter 5 ★ The Presidential Campaign 54

Chapter 6 ★ Promoting the Message 66

Chapter 7 ★ The Presidential Candidate 76

SERIES GLOSSARY OF KEY TERMS 88

FURTHER READING & INTERNET RESOURCES 92

INDEX 95

CREDITS 96

Key Icons to Look For

Words to Understand: These words with their easy-to-understand definitions will increase readers' understanding of the text while building vocabulary skills.

Sidebars: This boxed material within the main text allows readers to build knowledge, gain insights, explore possibilities, and broaden their perspectives by weaving together additional information to provide realistic and holistic perspectives.

Educational Videos: Readers can view videos by scanning our QR codes, providing them with additional educational content to supplement the text.

Text-Dependent Questions: These questions send the reader back to the text for more careful attention to the evidence presented there.

Research Projects: Readers are pointed toward areas of further inquiry connected to each chapter. Suggestions are provided for projects that encourage deeper research and analysis.

Series Glossary of Key Terms: This back-of-the-book glossary contains terminology used throughout this series. Words found here increase the reader's ability to read and comprehend higher-level books and articles in this field.

INTRODUCTION

The Evolving American Experiment

From the start, Americans have regarded their government with a mixture of reliance and mistrust. The men who founded the republic did not doubt the indispensability of government. "If men were angels," observed the 51st *Federalist Paper*, "no government would be necessary." But men are not angels. Because human beings are subject to wicked as well as to noble impulses, government was deemed essential to ensure freedom and order.

At the same time, the American revolutionaries knew that government could also become a source of injury and oppression. The men who gathered in Philadelphia in 1787 to write the Constitution therefore had two purposes in mind. They wanted to establish a strong central authority and to limit that central authority's capacity to abuse its power.

To prevent the abuse of power, the Founding Fathers wrote two basic principles into the new Constitution. The principle of federalism divided power between the state governments and the central authority. The principle of the separation of powers subdivided the central authority itself into three branches—the executive, the legislative, and the judiciary—so that "each may be a check on the other."

The Constitution did not plan the executive branch in any detail. After vesting the executive power in the president, it assumed the existence of "executive departments" without specifying what these departments should be. Congress began defining their functions in 1789 by creating the Departments of State, Treasury, and War. The secretaries in charge of these departments made up President Washington's first cabinet. Congress also provided for a legal officer, and President Washington soon invited the attorney general, as he was called, to attend cabinet meetings. As need required, Congress created more executive departments.

Setting up the cabinet was only the first step in organizing the American state. With almost no guidance from the Constitution, President Washington, seconded by Alexander Hamilton, his brilliant secretary of the treasury, equipped the infant republic with a working administrative structure. The Federalists believed in both executive energy and executive accountability and set high standards for public appointments. The Jeffersonian opposition had less faith in strong government and preferred local government to the central authority. But when Jefferson himself became president in 1801, although he set out to change the direction of policy, he found no reason to alter the framework the Federalists had erected.

By 1801, there were about 3,000 federal civilian employees in a nation of a little more than 5 million people. Growth in territory and population steadily enlarged national responsibilities. Thirty years later, when Jackson was president, there were more than 11,000 government workers in a nation of 13 million. The federal establishment was increasing at a rate faster than the population.

Jackson's presidency brought significant changes in the federal service. Jackson believed that the executive branch contained too many officials who saw their jobs as "species of property" and as "a means of promoting individual interest." Against the idea of a permanent service based on life tenure, Jackson argued for the periodic redistribution of federal offices, contending that this was the democratic way and that official duties could be made "so plain and simple that men of intelligence may readily qualify themselves for their performance." He called this policy *rotation-in-office*. His opponents called it the *spoils system*.

The United States Constitution has been the supreme law of the United States since its signing in 1787. Its first three words, "We the People," affirm that the government is here to serve the people.

In fact, partisan legend exaggerated the extent of Jackson's removals. More than 80 percent of federal officeholders retained their jobs. Jackson discharged no larger a proportion of government workers than Jefferson had done a generation earlier. But the rise in these years of mass political parties gave federal patronage new importance as a means of building the party and of rewarding activists. Jackson's successors were less restrained in the distribution of spoils. As the federal establishment grew—to nearly 40,000 by 1861—the politicization of the public service excited increasing concern.

After the Civil War, the spoils system became a major political issue. Highminded men condemned it as the root of all political evil. The spoilsmen, said the British commentator James Bryce, "have distorted and depraved the mechanism of politics." Patronage—giving jobs to unqualified, incompetent, and dishonest persons—lowered the standards of public service and nourished corrupt political machines. Office-seekers pursued presidents and cabinet secretaries without mercy. "Patronage," said Ulysses S. Grant after his presidency, "is the bane of the presidential office." "Every time I appoint someone to office," said another political leader, "I make a hundred enemies and one ingrate." George William Curtis, the president of the National Civil Service Reform League, summed up the indictment:

> The theory which perverts public trusts into party spoils, making public employment dependent upon personal favor and not on proved merit, necessarily ruins the self-respect of public employees, destroys the function of party in a republic, prostitutes elections into a desperate strife for personal profit, and degrades the national character by lowering the moral tone and standard of the country.

The object of civil service reform was to promote efficiency and honesty in the public service and to bring about the ethical regeneration of public life. In 1883, over bitter opposition from politicians, the reformers passed the Pendleton Act, establishing a bipartisan Civil Service Commission, competitive examinations, and appointment on merit. The Pendleton Act also gave the president authority to extend by executive order the number of "classified" jobs—that is, jobs subject to the merit system. The act applied initially only to about 14,000 of the more than 100,000 federal positions. But by the end of the nineteenth century, 40 percent of federal jobs had moved into the classified category.

The twentieth century saw a considerable expansion of the federal establishment. The Great Depression and the New Deal led the national government to take on a variety of new responsibilities. The New Deal extended the federal regulatory apparatus. By 1940, in a nation of 130 million people, the number of federal workers for the first time passed the 1 million mark. The Second World War brought federal civilian employment to 3.8 million in 1945. With peace, the federal establishment declined to around 2 million by 1950. Then growth resumed, reaching 2.8 million by the 1980s. In 2017, there were only 2.1 million federal civilian employees.

The New Deal years saw rising criticism of "big government" and "bureaucracy." Businessmen resented federal regulation. Conservatives worried about the impact of paternalistic government on individual self-reliance, on community responsibility, and on economic and personal freedom. The nation, in effect, renewed the old debate between Hamilton and Jefferson in the early republic.

Since the 1980s, with the presidency of Ronald Reagan, this debate has burst out with unusual intensity. According to conservatives, government intervention abridges liberty, stifles enterprise, and is inefficient, wasteful, and arbitrary. It disturbs the harmony of the self-adjusting market and creates worse troubles than it solves. "Get government off our backs," according to the popular cliché, and our problems will solve themselves. When government is necessary, let it be at the local level, close to the people.

In fact, for all the talk about the "swollen" and "bloated" bureaucracy, the federal establishment has not been growing as inexorably as many Americans seem to believe. In 1949, it consisted of 2.1 million people. Nearly 70 years later, while the country had grown by 177 million, the federal force is the same. Federal workers were a smaller percentage of the population in 2017 than they were in 1985, 1955, or 1940. The federal establishment, in short, has not kept pace with population growth. Moreover, national defense and security-related agencies account for nearly 70 percent of federal employment.

Why, then, the widespread idea about the remorseless growth of government? It is partly because in the 1960s, the national government assumed new and intrusive functions: affirmative action in civil rights, environmental protection, safety and health in the workplace, community organization, legal aid to the poor. Although this enlargement of the federal regulatory role was accompanied by marked growth in the size of government on all levels, the expansion has taken place primarily in state and local government. Whereas the federal force increased by only 27 percent in the 30 years after 1950, the state and local government forces increased by an astonishing 212 percent.

In general, Americans do not want less government. What they want is *more efficient* government. For a time in the 1970s, with the Vietnam War and Watergate, Americans lost confidence in the national government. In 1964, more than three-quarters of those polled had thought the national government could be trusted to do right most of the time. By 1980, only one-quarter was prepared to offer such trust. After reaching a three-decade high in the wake of the 9/11 terrorist attacks, public confidence in the federal government was near historic lows in 2017 at just 18 percent.

Two hundred years after the drafting of the Constitution, Americans still regard government with a mixture of reliance and mistrust—a good combination. Mistrust is the best way to keep government reliable. Informed criticism is the means of correcting governmental inefficiency, incompetence, and arbitrariness; that is, of best enabling government to play its essential role. For without government, we cannot attain the goals of the Founding Fathers. Without an understanding of government, we cannot have the informed criticism that makes government do the job right. It is the duty of every American citizen to know our government—which is what this series is all about.

Too Close to Call

Words to Understand

Ambassador: A person who acts as the representative of a nation, organization, or other group in discussions or negotiations with others.

Policy maker: A government official or member of an organization who participates in the shaping of laws.

Recount: In election terminology, when the results of a close vote are counted again to ensure they are correct.

Election Day, November 7, 2000: The day on which Americans would choose their next president began in typical fashion. The two candidates—Republican George W. Bush and Democrat Al Gore—had returned to their home districts (in Texas and Tennessee, respectively) to cast their votes. Each had spent the past several months crisscrossing the country in an effort to persuade voters that he would be the best person to serve as the 43rd president of the United States.

The campaign had been a close one, with different polls showing one or the other candidate narrowly leading the race for the presidency. The two men had certain factors in common. They both were the sons of famous politicians, for whom they had been named—Al Gore's father, Albert Gore Sr., had been an influential U.S. senator from Tennessee, whereas George

In 1993, Bill Clinton stood in front of thousands as he took the oath of office of the president of the United States. In eight years' time, he would hand the torch over to the next president-elect. No one knew how tumultuous the process leading up to that handover would be.

W. Bush was the son of the 41st president, George H.W. Bush. Both men had grown up in powerful political circles. Al Gore spent much of his childhood in Washington, D.C. His family had a penthouse there, in the Fairfax Hotel, where his father would meet with presidents and **policy makers**. George W. Bush's grandfather, Prescott Bush, had served as a U.S. senator from Connecticut; before he became president, George H.W. Bush had served as a United Nations **ambassador**, the director of the Central Intelligence Agency, and the vice president under Ronald Reagan.

Both of the candidates had attended top universities. Al Gore was a graduate of Harvard University. George W. Bush was a Yale University graduate and had earned an MBA from Harvard University. They were close in age: Al Gore was 52 years old at the time of the election, whereas George W. Bush was 54. Finally, each man deeply and strongly believed that he was the better man to become the next president of the United States.

There were important differences between the two men, however, which divided the country during this election year. After graduating from college, Al Gore had enlisted to serve in the war in Vietnam, despite his personal opposition to the conflict, and had spent much of the war working as an army journalist. At the age of 28, he ran for, and was elected to, the U.S. House of Representatives, the same position that his father had once held. After eight years, he was elected to the U.S. Senate.

As a U.S. senator from Tennessee, Gore focused on issues involving arms control and technology. Unlike many other Democrats, Gore supported President George H.W. Bush's decision to send troops to fight against Iraq in Operation Desert Storm, as well as in a military intervention in the conflict in Bosnia. After his failed first run for the Democratic presidential nomination in 1988, Gore wrote a best-selling book that focused on environmental issues, and he later served as vice president in Bill Clinton's administration.

Gore had been a visible vice president, working closely with President Clinton. That closeness had become a liability when Clinton's administration was caught up in questions about fund-raising methods and scandals involving Clinton's personal life. Gore was also criticized for appearing wooden and dull in speeches and at public appearances.

Gore's opponent, Texas governor George W. Bush, described himself as a "compassionate conservative" during the 2000 campaign. After a time in college during which he was, in his own words, "young and irresponsible," he joined the Texas National Guard as a pilot. This would prove problematic during his campaign, with some suggesting that the Bush family had used their connections to obtain a

The 2000 presidential race between Republican candidate George W. Bush and Democratic candidate Al Gore was one of the closest races in U.S. history. Even though more Americans voted for Al Gore, George W. Bush won the majority of the electoral votes, making him the 43rd president of the United States. In the aftermath of the election, voters for both candidates showed their support at rallies across the country.

spot for George W. in the National Guard to prevent him from being drafted to fight in Vietnam.

After earning a master's degree in business administration, Bush made money in the oil industry and bought a stake in a professional baseball team. He ran for Congress but was not elected. He did not seek further political office until after his father's presidency. Then he ran for governor of Texas and was elected.

As governor, Bush made major improvements in the state's school systems, dramatically expanded Texas's prison system, and opposed greater restrictions on guns. His presidential campaign focused in part on poverty, education, and minorities.

The campaign was hard fought and seemed close through Election Day. On that November 7, only about half of all eligible voters cast their ballots in the presidential election. Little did they know how important each vote would prove to be.

After polling booths closed on the East Coast, the television networks began airing predictions of the election results based on polls of voters as they left the places where they had voted. The state of Florida was considered to be a key state for the presidential candidates, but early results indicated that the election there was too close to call. Then, at 8:00 p.m., the television networks began to declare that Al Gore had won in Florida. Many felt that this was a sign that the Democrat would become the next president.

Other states began to fall to the candidates as expected. Pennsylvania and Michigan were declared to have been won by Gore; Ohio was a victory for Bush. Still, the Bush campaign refused to give up on Florida. Bush's brother, Jeb Bush, was the governor of Florida, and the Bush campaign's own polls suggested that the state might prove a victory for Bush rather than Gore.

Two hours after the television networks declared that Al Gore had won the state of Florida's electoral votes, network news anchors were forced to make an embarrassing announcement: The declaration had been premature; the election results in that state were too close to call.

As polling places closed across the country, each state became increasingly crucial. California, with its prized 54 electoral votes, went to Al Gore, as did Iowa. The networks—and the campaigns—tallied up the electoral votes belonging to each candidate. Neither one had yet received enough electoral votes to be declared the winner. It all came down to one state: Florida. Whoever won Florida would win the presidential election.

Finally, two hours and 20 minutes after voting ended in Alaska, the television networks once again made an announcement: Florida had been won by George W.

Bush. This meant that he would become the 43rd president of the United States. Twenty minutes after the announcement, Al Gore phoned George Bush to concede (officially admit defeat) and congratulate his opponent on winning the election. After a long election night, many Americans went to bed believing that George W. Bush had been declared the winner and that the election was over. They were wrong.

Uncertainty and Chaos

Shortly after phoning his opponent, Al Gore learned that the results of the election in Florida were so close that state law required an automatic **recount** of the votes. That state was not yet officially granting its electoral votes to either candidate and would not do so until the results of the recount were known.

Within 30 minutes of his first call, Al Gore again phoned George Bush, this time to tell him that he was withdrawing his concession. George W. Bush was shocked. He could not believe that this was happening.

Footage from the 2000 election.

For the next month, the question of who would become the 43rd president of the United States went unanswered. Attention focused on the state of Florida as individual counties began the tedious process of recounting the votes. In some instances, these votes were recounted manually (by hand); lawyers then questioned whether these manual recounts were constitutional. There were reports of voting machines failing to register a vote accurately, leaving voting officials to study the ballots to determine whether a voter had attempted to vote for a particular candidate.

Once the courts had resolved the question of whether manual recounts were constitutional and could proceed (the legal ruling was that they could), other legal questions arose. The Democrats challenged a deadline imposed by the Florida courts for completing the recount process. Next came the deadline at which Florida was required by law to award its electoral votes—December 12. That, too, passed without a winner being declared.

Both Democrats and Republicans accused their opponents of interfering with the election results. Republicans suggested that Al Gore was simply being a "sore loser," refusing to admit defeat. Democrats suggested that Republicans were attempting to stop the recounts so that their candidate would be declared the winner.

The case was appealed to higher and higher courts as the recounts proceeded and were periodically halted. The Florida Supreme Court had ruled that manual recounts were allowed and that all questionable ballots in the state should be recounted by hand. The Bush campaign appealed this decision, however. The case finally reached the U.S. Supreme Court.

It was an extraordinary legal moment. The U.S. Supreme Court was, in a sense, being pitted against the Florida Supreme Court. It was also going to be put in the position, through its ruling, of having a direct impact on who would become the next president of the United States.

Like much of the country, the nine U.S. Supreme Court justices had divided opinions over whether the manual recounts were constitutional. Seven of the nine justices, however, ruled that there were constitutional problems with the recount as ordered by the Florida Supreme Court. The Court also ruled (in a narrower majority of five to four) that there was no constitutionally acceptable procedure that would allow a recount to take place before the deadline at which the state's electors had to be chosen (the procedure by which the state's electoral votes would officially be awarded). The U.S. Supreme Court based this decision on its concern that different standards for the recounts were being used in the different Florida counties, which might result in unequal treatment for the candidates.

AN ADVISER'S ANALYSIS

Stanley Greenberg, an adviser to Al Gore's 2000 campaign, has suggested that Gore's defeat in the presidential election was attributable in part to his role as vice president to Bill Clinton. In Greenberg's view, the vice presidency can be a difficult role, particularly when one is serving under a popular president. The vice president is easily overshadowed by the president and finds it difficult to claim credit for an administration's accomplishments (these are usually credited to the president), but is held responsible for an administration's failings. Bill Clinton's second term in office was tarnished by personal scandals. According to Greenberg, they contributed to Gore's defeat.

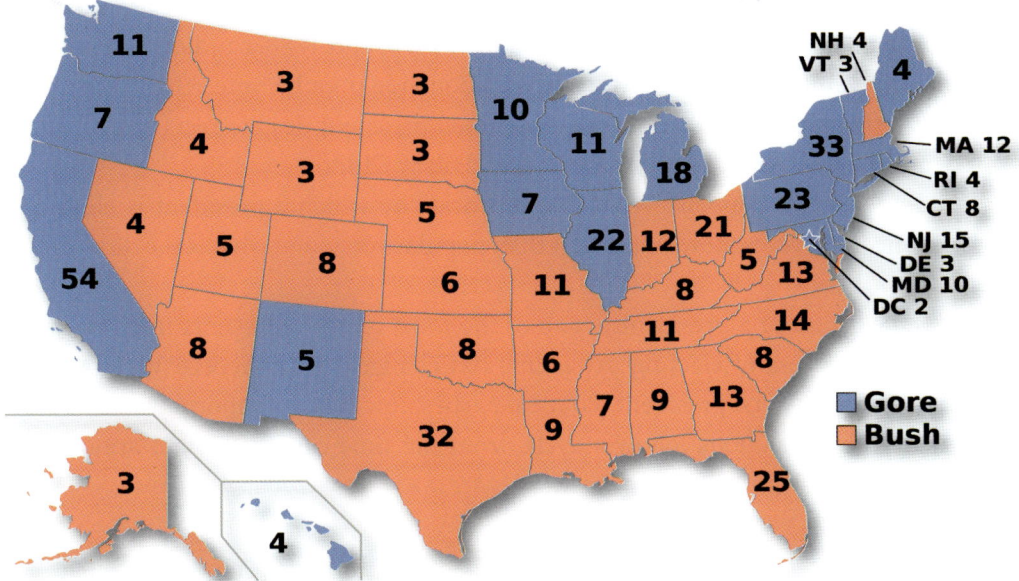

The map pictured above shows the electoral votes cast for each state in the 2000 presidential election.

The ruling—which did not give the Florida court time to fix the situation by setting recount standards to be used across the state—meant that the recount process was halted. Al Gore once again conceded, noting that he disagreed with the ruling by the U.S. Supreme Court but urging Americans to support George Bush. After 36 days, the winner of the 2000 presidential election was finally declared.

The Result

Votes were cast in the 2000 presidential election on November 7, but it was not until December 13 that George W. Bush could publicly claim the presidency. "I was elected not to serve one party but one nation," he announced in his long-postponed victory speech.

In the end, the question of who would become the next president hinged on a few hundred votes in Florida. The election would prove to be one of the closest in U.S. history. It would also prove notable for another reason: George W. Bush was declared the 43rd president of the United States, even though more Americans had voted for Al Gore.

It was not the first time that a candidate had become president even though his opponent had received more votes. In 1824, 1876, and 1888, candidates won the presidency even though they had lost the nationwide popular vote. This happened again in 2016, when Donald Trump was elected president despite receiving almost three million votes fewer than his challenger, Hilary Clinton.

How can this happen? What is the process by which a president is elected? Why are electoral votes more important than popular votes, and what is the difference between the two?

The election of a president is one of the most important events in American politics. The process of electing presidents has changed since George Washington became the nation's first president. Political parties now play an important role in the election process. Elections follow a cycle, from the time candidates first announce

After a tumultuous battle in 2000, President Bush won his second term in the 2004 election. On January 20, 2005, George W. Bush was inaugurated for his second term as president of the United States. In the photograph above, Bush addresses the crowd in front of the U.S. Capitol Building.

their intentions to run for the presidency, through the primary season, and on to the national election. Campaigns dramatically impact voters' impressions of the candidates. Election practices have changed over the more than 200 years of American history, as have the particular skills, background, and experience necessary to become the president of the United States.

Text-Dependent Questions

1. Name two ways in which Al Gore and George W. Bush had similar upbringings.

2. Did the Florida Supreme Court rule that manual recounts were allowed after the 2000 election?

3. Did more Americans vote for George W. Bush or Al Gore in the 2000 election?

Research Project

Research one of the presidential elections in which the winning candidate lost the popular vote. Write a brief report outlining the biographies of the candidates, the circumstances of the election and its key issues, how the election was ultimately decided, and the reactions of the candidates and public.

Too Close to Call

2

Electing a President

Words to Understand

Amendment: An addition or change to a document.
Delegate: A person dispatched to represent others at a conference, legislative session, or other official event.
Monarchy: A government ruled by a single person such as a king or queen, who usually inherits his or her power.

When the members of the Constitutional Convention gathered in Philadelphia in 1787, they were faced with a nearly overwhelming challenge: How should the new nation be governed? The decisions made by those **delegates** shaped the U.S. government, which was divided into three branches—the executive, the legislative, and the judicial. These decision-makers also determined how the men and women who served in those branches of government would be chosen.

The executive branch of government sparked particularly intense debate. Most delegates were clearest about the form of leadership they did not want: Only recently, they had successfully fought and won their liberty from Great Britain, and they wanted to be sure not to create another **monarchy**. Some delegates favored the idea of an executive branch formed of several people, each with a different area of expertise. Others supported an executive branch that reported to Congress, with

The first flag was raised at Independence Hall in Philadelphia in 1776. Nearly 10 years later, the first Constitutional Convention would be held to determine how the new nation should be governed.

Congress deciding what tasks the executive would handle and how many people would be needed.

Eventually, however, under a proposal known as the Virginia Plan (authored, most believe, by James Madison), the delegates began to consider the idea of a single chief executive or president, who would serve for a specific period of time. Under the Virginia Plan, the president was to be chosen by Congress and would serve one seven-year term.

The idea of having a president chosen by Congress was troubling to some of the delegates, however. It seemed to contradict the original reason for creating three separate branches of government: to guarantee a balance of power and a certain amount of independence for each division of the government. By having one of the branches (the executive) appointed by another (the legislative), the balance of power would shift and place too much power in the hands of Congress.

The delegates wanted to ensure that the president was truly a representative of the people. This was a good reason for the president to be selected by the people's representatives (Congress). The idea of having the president chosen by popular vote of all American citizens did not seem practical to the delegates; in those days, before instant communication and political campaigns, they worried that citizens would not have the information necessary to assess the strengths and weaknesses of the candidates. In addition, the size of the country and the distances among the states made it difficult to oversee and determine the results of a national election.

After much debate, the delegates decided to create an electoral college—a group of representatives from each state who would meet and vote for a particular candidate. Under the original plan, the candidate who received the majority of the votes from the Electoral College would be elected president. The one with the second highest total would become vice president.

According to the Constitution

When the Constitutional Convention ended, its delegates had drafted a document that formed the basis for the government of the United States. As the country has evolved, so, too, has the Constitution, and **amendments** have been added to reflect the demands of a changing nation and its people.

Several sections of the Constitution concern the presidency and how a president is elected. Article II, Section 1, states: "The executive power shall be vested in

In 1787, 55 delegates from several states convened in Philadelphia for the Constitutional Convention. It was there that they drafted a document that would be the basis for the government of the United States. This painting by Howard Chandler, Scene at the Signing of the Constitution, *hangs in the United States Capitol Building.*

a President of the United States of America. He shall hold his office during the term of four years. . . ." It specifies the system for choosing the president—the Electoral College—and the qualifications necessary to be president: "No person except a natural born citizen, or a citizen of the United States, at the time of the adoption of this Constitution, shall be eligible to the office of President; neither shall any person be eligible to that office who shall not have attained to the age of thirty five years, and been fourteen years a resident within the United States."

This basic framework has served as a solid foundation on which the American presidency is shaped. Over the years, however, additional amendments have been added to the Constitution to reflect changes in the system for electing the president.

In 1804, the Twelfth Amendment to the Constitution was adopted; it significantly changed the system used for electing the president. This amendment was a response to the difficulties surrounding the presidential election of 1800.

In that election, an equal number of votes were cast in the Electoral College for Thomas Jefferson and Aaron Burr in an effort to ensure that they were elected president and vice president, respectively. The result, of course, was a tie. The House of Representatives was forced to decide the outcome of the election, and it took several days and 36 ballots before Jefferson was elected president.

The Twelfth Amendment requires separate votes for president and vice president, a change from the previous system, in which the person receiving the second highest number of votes for president became vice president. The amendment also states that when they vote, the electors must choose a president and a vice president from different states. It is for this reason that, even today, presidential and vice-presidential candidates are never from the same state.

The Fifteenth Amendment (1870) made it clear that race could not be an issue in denying citizens the right to vote. It stated: "The right of citizens of the United States to vote shall not be denied or abridged by the United States or by any state on account of race, color, or previous condition of servitude."

With the Nineteenth Amendment (1920), the right to vote was extended to women. In the amendment's language, "The right of citizens of the United States to vote shall not be denied or abridged by the United States or by any state on account of sex."

Finally, the Twenty-Sixth Amendment (1971) lowered the age for citizens to vote from 21 to 18: "The right of citizens of the United States, who are 18 years of age or older, to vote, shall not be denied or abridged by the United States or by any state on account of age."

The First Election

The Founding Fathers envisioned that the members of the Electoral College would be educated, wealthy, and prominent, and that they would carefully study and debate the qualifications of the various candidates before deciding which one would make the best president. The creation of political parties, the increase of public participation in an election, and the advent of conventions, campaigns, and public scrutiny of candidates has dramatically transformed what was intended to be a careful, deliberative process into what can, at times, seem like a carnival.

This was clearly not the case when the Constitution was written. Even as the delegates to the Constitutional Convention outlined their plans for the new government and the office of the presidency, it became evident that George Washington,

In the presidential election of 1800, Thomas Jefferson tied with his opponent, Aaron Burr (shown here), for the most votes. The decision went to the House of Representatives, and Jefferson became the third president of the United States. Following this controversial election, the Twelfth Amendment was added to the Constitution.

president of the Constitutional Convention and victorious general in the Revolutionary War, would be the obvious choice for the nation's first president. Washington was certainly not the last president who would owe his election to success on the battlefield, but it is to his credit that, as the nation's first president, he also remains one of its best.

Although Washington was the unanimous choice for the first American president, it is interesting to note that he was not the only candidate to receive votes. In the somewhat awkward system initially conceived for electing the president, members of the Electoral College needed to cast two votes for president; as mentioned earlier, the man receiving the second highest number of votes was then

THE ELECTION OF 1789

George Washington was the unanimous choice of the electors who cast their ballots in the presidential election of 1789—the only president to have been elected unanimously. At the time, members of the Electoral College were required to vote twice—the candidate who received the most votes would become president, and the second place candidate would become vice president. A total of 69 electors voted for the president in 1789.

Candidate	Electoral Votes Received
George Washington	69
John Adams	34
John Jay	9
John Rutledge	6
Robert Harrison	6
John Hancock	4
George Clinton	3
Others	7

chosen as vice president. George Washington received one vote from every member of the Electoral College, for a total of 69 electoral votes. Other candidates receiving votes included John Adams of Massachusetts (whose 34 electoral votes qualified him to serve as vice president), John Jay of New York, John Rutledge of South Carolina, Robert Harrison of Maryland, John Hancock of Massachusetts, and George Clinton of New York. Washington remains the only president ever to have been elected unanimously by the Electoral College.

George Washington took his oath of office in New York City on April 30, 1789. New York served as the capital of the United States for 18 months before the seat of government was relocated to Philadelphia. This provided Washington with yet another distinction from the presidents who would serve after him: He is the only president never to live in Washington, D.C., during his presidency.

The inauguration of George Washington.

There was much about the concept of the presidency that was new at the time, and much about the office that was permanently shaped by George Washington. Washington was actively involved in both foreign and domestic policy. He confidently assumed the title of commander-in-chief of the military. He decided to serve no more than two terms as president, although it is likely that he could have remained as president for life had he chosen to do so. Future presidents—with the exception of Franklin D. Roosevelt, who was elected to four terms as president—would follow his example, and the Twenty-Second Amendment to the Constitution, ratified in 1951, limited presidents after Roosevelt to two terms.

Washington, as the first president, would remain a model for others who would be elected to the office. Military service would be viewed as an asset for many future presidents. Four of the nation's first five presidents would all be, like Washington, from Virginia—the exception was John Adams, who had been Washington's vice president. Washington also lobbied hard for the nation's new permanent capital to be located conveniently near his home, Mount Vernon, in Virginia.

George Washington was the first president of the United States. Elected in 1789, Washington served two terms as president until 1797. Since 1951, the Twenty-Second Amendment to the Constitution has limited presidents to two terms.

Important Elections

Other elections have affected how future presidents are chosen. As mentioned earlier, in the election of 1800, Thomas Jefferson and Aaron Burr tied for the presidency. This was caused by the efforts of electors who were members of the

Democratic-Republican Party. Eager to ensure that their party controlled both the presidency and vice presidency (and to force John Adams and his Federalist Party out of office), the Democratic-Republican electors cast an equal number of votes for Jefferson and Burr. The election was then given to the House of Representatives to decide. Jefferson was ultimately chosen as president, and Burr as his vice president, and the Twelfth Amendment, passed in 1804, ensured that separate votes would be cast for president and vice president in the future.

The House of Representatives decided a presidential election once more, in 1824: Following the election, no candidate had won a majority of the electoral votes. At 99 votes, Andrew Jackson had received the most, whereas John Quincy Adams had 84; William H. Crawford, 41; and Henry Clay, 37. By 1824, electors were being chosen in 18 of the then-24 states by popular vote, and Jackson also led in the popular vote.

Because no candidate had received a majority, the House of Representatives was ordered to choose the winner. According to the Twelfth Amendment, only the top three contenders would be considered, which meant Jackson, Adams, and Crawford. But Crawford, who had served as secretary of the treasury under President James Monroe, had suffered a serious illness, which made it unlikely that he would be able to effectively serve as president. This narrowed the House's choice down to two—Jackson and Adams—and meant that whoever won the support of Clay would gain his electoral votes and the presidency.

Both sides lobbied hard to win Clay's support, but it was John Quincy Adams who won the support and the votes in the House. Jackson was outraged by the results, believing that, since he had received more electoral and popular votes, he should have been chosen as president. He hinted that some sort of deal had been made between Adams and Clay, a charge that seemed accurate when, shortly after the election was finalized, Adams appointed Clay as his secretary of state. The charge of election rigging against his opponent would help increase Jackson's popularity and propel him into the White House four years later.

The election of 1836 offers another example of how the system for electing the president is continuously changing. In that election, the Whig Party decided to run different presidential candidates in different parts of the country, with the idea that each candidate could win votes for the Whig Party in the region where he was the strongest candidate. The Whig electors would then choose the best candidate to serve as president, or the election could be decided in the House of Representatives. As a result, William Henry Harrison ran as the Whig candidate in most of

New England, Daniel Webster was the Whig candidate in Massachusetts, and Hugh White (from Tennessee) was the Whig candidate in the South. It would have been an interesting strategy had it proved effective, but the only result of this divide-and-conquer plan was that the Democratic nominee, Martin Van Buren, was able to capture a majority of the electoral votes.

William Henry Harrison was the Whig candidate in the presidential election of 1836.

Text-Dependent Questions

1. Under what proposal did delegates to the Constitutional Convention begin to consider the idea of a single chief executive or president?

2. What does the Twelfth Amendment require?

3. Why was the House of Representatives ordered to choose the winner of the 1824 election?

Research Project

Research the Fifteenth, Nineteenth, or Twenty-Sixth Amendment, which all extended voting rights to new groups of American citizens. Write a brief report outlining the historical background of the amendment; key figures who lobbied on its behalf; the path of its ratification, including struggles and opposition it might have faced; and how it impacted American political life.

3

The Electoral College

Words to Understand

Formality: Something that is done purely to meet an established custom or requirement.
Legislature: The assembly of a government or state that is tasked with making laws.
Tabulate: To count or record data.

On four different occasions, the man who was elected president of the United States lost the popular vote. How is it possible that a candidate can receive fewer votes than his opponent, yet still win the presidency?

The reason for this is the system of voting known as the Electoral College. The Electoral College was first proposed during the 1787 Constitutional Convention as the best solution to the problem of how the president should be elected. The idea of a popular vote, in which citizens chose the president, did not seem practical; in those early years of a scattered population, it seemed unlikely that citizens would be familiar with all of the candidates, and so would vote for the candidate they knew best, giving an advantage to candidates from heavily populated states.

In the 2016 presidential election, Donald Trump lost the popular vote but won in the Electoral College, ultimately defeating Hillary Clinton.

HOW THE PRESIDENT IS ELECTED

The Constitutional Convention appointed 11 of their delegates to a special committee, designed to solve the problem of how best to choose the president. This "Committee of 11" proposed a compromise: A "college of electors" would be formed. (In this context, *college* means simply "an organized group of people.") Each state would be granted a certain number of electors, based on the total number of senators (for all states, two) and representatives (varying by state). Each state would determine how its electors would be chosen. A presidential candidate would need to win a majority (one more than one-half) of the votes in the Electoral College; if he failed to do so, the election would be decided in the House of Representatives (initially, the Committee of 11 felt it should be decided in the Senate, but this was changed to the House of Representatives), with each state given one vote.

With the Electoral College, even the smallest states were given a role in deciding the outcome of presidential elections. They would have at least three electoral votes—two for their senators and one for each representative. The system also gave the individual states great power in determining how and when their electors would be chosen.

Many experts agree that the drafters of the Constitution believed that most presidential candidates after George Washington would fail to win a majority of the Electoral College votes. According to this view, the Electoral College would provide an initial weeding out of candidates; when none of them won a majority of the votes, the top five candidates would be considered in the House of Representatives. Each state would be given one vote, which would ensure that each state, regardless of its size, would have an equal say in the election.

Other steps were taken in the creation of the Electoral College to ensure fairness and balance. To avoid one branch of the government becoming too powerful, members of Congress and employees of the federal government could not serve as electors. Each state's electors were to meet in their individual states rather than in a large central gathering of all electors; this provision was designed to prevent making secret deals or outside influence on an election. Each elector was required to cast two votes for president, and one of those votes had to be for someone from a different state. This was done to prevent electors from voting only for candidates from their own states. The belief was that the eventual choice as president would often be the second choice of many of the voters. The electoral votes from each state would be sealed and delivered to the president of the Senate, who would then appear before a joint meeting of the Senate and House of Representatives and read the results.

The System Changes

Created before political parties and campaigns, the Electoral College was conceived as a system where educated, thoughtful delegates would meet and carefully debate the qualifications of a candidate before casting their votes. The election of 1800 forced a change in the system, however. The tie between Thomas Jefferson and Aaron Burr had resulted in intense behind-the-scenes campaigning and making deals and required 36 separate ballots before a winner was determined. The tie had also been caused by the rising influence of political parties; Democratic-Republican supporters of Jefferson and Burr were so desperate to ensure that the Federalist candidates were defeated that they had intentionally created a tie.

The secret maneuvering that finally resulted in Jefferson's election was precisely the kind of activity that the Founding Fathers had hoped to prevent with the creation of the Electoral College. With the Twelfth Amendment, the Electoral College system was changed so that electors voted separately for president and vice president.

Other changes in the Electoral College took place that altered it even further from the original idea of the Committee of 11. Many of these changes were attributable to the growing role played by political parties. The initial plan was for the members of the Electoral College to be among the most distinguished citizens of each state. But with the rise of political parties, delegates to the Electoral College were increasingly chosen not for their prominence in their state, but for their loyalty to their political party. Today, the names of few delegates to the Electoral College would be recognized, even in their home states. They are not the free voters imagined by the Constitution but instead are expected to vote according to the regulations governing electors in their individual states.

In a presidential election, when you cast your vote, you are voting not for the candidates for president and vice president but instead for the electors for that candidate. The words "electors for" generally appear in small print before the names of the candidates for vice president and president. Whichever party's ticket wins the most popular votes in a state wins that states' electors, with only two exceptions: Maine and Nebraska. In those two states, two electors are chosen by statewide popular vote, and the remainder are chosen by popular vote within each congressional district.

This represents a significant change in the Electoral College system as it was initially imagined. Instead of a body of prominent, independent citizens who

Casting your vote in a presidential election means you are casting a vote for the electors, not the candidates.

thoughtfully consider the various candidates, it has instead become a system where unknown delegates automatically cast their votes for a particular candidate based on the results of a popular election.

Another such change affected the idea that the Electoral College would provide an initial screening or nominating process for candidates, with the final results of elections being decided in the House of Representatives. Rather than being a routine part of the process, a final decision in the House became a procedure used only in emergencies; inevitably, it would lead to bitter disagreement, making deals, and division.

How Electors Are Chosen

The way in which electors to the Electoral College are chosen has also undergone change since the first presidential election. Initially, the system for choosing electors was left to the individual states. In some cases, state **legislatures** decided to choose the electors themselves. In other cases, a direct popular vote for electors was held, either by congressional district or across the entire state. In all of these cases, a list of different candidates was prepared, and the electors were chosen from that list.

In the 1800s, however, the system changed. By 1860, all states had determined to choose their electors by statewide popular election. Maine and Nebraska are the only two remaining exceptions; they, as noted earlier, choose two electors based on statewide popular vote and the remainder by popular vote in each congressional district.

The Electoral College also gradually shifted to what is called a "winner-take-all" system for choosing electors. This is the system in use today in the majority of the states. A candidate who wins a state's popular vote then almost always wins all of that state's electors.

Similarly, the time for choosing electors has changed over the years. For the first 50 years, states were allowed to choose their electors—in essence, hold their presidential elections—at any time within a 34-day period before the first Wednesday of December. This first Wednesday was the day when electors were expected to meet in their individual states and choose their candidate for president. As the country grew, and our systems of communication developed, however, this election scheduling began to present problems. States could choose to hold their elections late in the 34-day period, waiting to see how candidates had performed in states that held their elections earlier. In close elections, states that voted at the end might determine the outcome, giving them an unfair advantage in choosing the president.

In 1845, Congress addressed this problem by setting a standard day on which all states were to choose their electors: the Tuesday following the first Monday in years that can be divided by four. That date remains the date on which all states hold their presidential elections. Each state's electoral college meets on the Monday following the second Wednesday of December in its state capital and casts its electoral votes—one for president and one for vice president. This second step has become more of a **formality** in recent years though. With modern communication, the results of a popular election are quickly **tabulated**, and the number of electors for a particular candidate are publicized well before the Electoral College meets.

Challenging Elections

There have been several elections in which the Electoral College system contributed to confusion or dramatically affected the outcome. The election of 1800 has already been discussed, as has the election of 1824, in which the House of Representatives ultimately chose John Quincy Adams as president. The election of 1836, in which the Whig Party ran three separate candidates for president and lost to Democratic-Republican candidate Martin Van Buren, was also covered.

In 1872, Republican president Ulysses S. Grant ran for re-election. His challenger was Democratic candidate Horace Greeley, a prominent journalist who had made famous the phrase "Go West, young man!" The problem arose when Greeley died in the period between the popular election that chose electors and the December meeting of the Electoral College. The electors pledged to Greeley were then faced with the awkward situation of determining whether or not to cast their electoral votes for a dead man. Strangely enough, three electors did. The others cast their votes for several other Democratic candidates. The outcome was not really significant, because Grant had won a majority of the electors, but still, it was a strange challenge to the Electoral College system.

The election of 1876 presented another set of problems. In that election, Republican candidate Rutherford B. Hayes ran against Democrat Samuel Tilden. The initial results suggested that Tilden had won; he had strong support in Southern states and had also gained the votes of Indiana, New York, Connecticut, and New Jersey. Tilden led in the popular vote by more than 250,000. Questions soon arose, however, about the votes in South Carolina, Florida, and Louisiana. In the period between the popular vote and the meeting of the electors in each state, supporters of the two candidates intensely lobbied the states' electors. In the end, each state delivered two sets of electoral votes, one set for Tilden and the other for Hayes.

Congress appointed a special 15-member commission to determine how each of the three states' electoral votes should be awarded. Again, intense lobbying and making deals followed, and in the end, the commission awarded each of the three states' electoral votes to Hayes. As a result, Hayes was elected president, with 185 electoral votes to Tilden's 184. In 1887, Congress passed special legislation designed to determine how to handle electoral votes in the event of a dispute, to ensure that the events of the 1876 election could not be repeated.

Famous journalist and newspaper editor Horace Greeley (left) ran for U.S. president in 1872 against incumbent Ulysses S. Grant (right). Greeley died before electoral votes could be cast. Ulysses S. Grant won the election and remained in office for a second term.

The election of 1888 offers an example in which a presidential candidate lost the popular vote by a significant margin and yet, because of votes in the Electoral College, won the presidency. In that election, President Grover Cleveland, a Democrat, won a large majority of the votes in the 18 states that supported him. Republican Benjamin Harrison won 20 states but only by very narrow margins. Yet, Harrison's 20 states gave him 233 electoral votes to Cleveland's 168, and so he became president.

A look at the 1888 election.

How the Electoral College Works Today

The Electoral College has evolved as a result of these challenges and changes, yet it is still the system by which our presidents are chosen. Today, each state is given a certain number of electors based on its senators (always two) and the number of its U.S. representatives. This second number varies by state and can change if a state's population changes significantly.

Major political parties choose their electors either through state party conventions or through state party leaders appointing the electors. The political parties in each state then give to their state's chief election official the list of electors who are

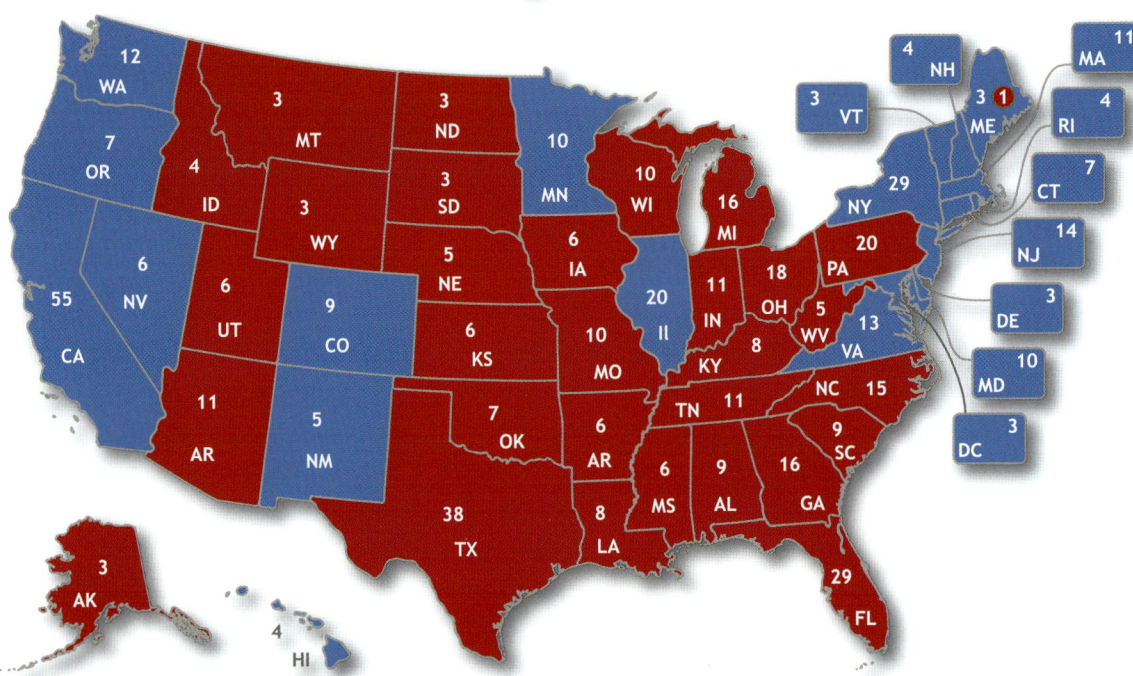

The Electoral College consists of officials from each state who vote for the president and vice president of the United States based on how their state's electorate voted. The map above shows the Electoral College voting in the 2016 presidential election.

pledged to vote for their party's candidate for president. This list is equal to the number of electoral votes a state has been given.

On the Tuesday following the first Monday in November in years that can be divided by four, the people cast their votes for the electors for a particular candidate for president and vice president. Whichever party wins the most popular votes in a state wins the electors of the state (with the exceptions of Maine and Nebraska, as noted earlier). On the Monday after the second Wednesday in December, each state's electors meet and cast their votes for president and vice president.

COLLEGE DEBATE

The Electoral College is a hotly debated topic, especially in the run-up to a presidential election. Critics say that the system does not truly represent the will of the people, as candidates who win the popular vote (i.e., the overall number of votes from citizens across the country) can still lose the election. In addition, states that are known to be traditionally Democratic or Republican offer less incentive for candidates to visit and win over individual voters; candidates focus a disproportionate amount of time on "swing states" that are not as reliably partisan. Finally, critics point to the fact that millions of individual votes are essentially "wasted," since no matter how large the margin of a candidate's victory is in a certain state, he or she will only receive a fixed amount of Electoral College votes.

Defenders of the Electoral College say that it prevents states with smaller populations from being dominated by populous states with large metropolitan areas. They also say that it prevents one region from determining the fate of the rest of the country, since voter representation is distributed throughout the states. While opinions are strong on both sides, it appears that the Electoral College will be the law of the land for the foreseeable future: Short of a constitutional amendment or another constitutional convention, it would be difficult to revise the system at this time.

The electoral votes are then sealed and transmitted to the president of the Senate, who opens them on January 6 and reads them before both houses of Congress. The candidate with the most electoral votes (it must be an absolute majority, or at least one more than half of the total) is declared president. If no one receives an absolute majority of the votes, the House of Representatives selects the candidate from among the top three candidates. Each state receives one vote; the candidate must receive an absolute majority to be elected. The president and vice president are then sworn into office at noon on January 20.

Although the Electoral College was initially intended to address the concern of smaller states that their voices might not carry weight in presidential elections, the reality is that certain heavily populated states are considered key to elections and receive intense focus during presidential campaigns. With 55, California has the largest number of electoral votes. Other states with large numbers of electoral votes include Texas (38), New York (29), Florida (29), Illinois and Pennsylvania (each with 20), and Ohio (18). The total number of electoral votes in the United States is 538; a candidate needs at least 270 electoral votes to win a presidential election.

Text-Dependent Questions

1. What was the reasoning behind the proposal of the Electoral College at the 1787 Constitutional Convention?

2. How are electors chosen in Maine and Nebraska?

3. True or false: The number of electors in a given state can never change.

Research Project

Research the Electoral College breakdown of the 2016 presidential election. Which states were highly contested for their electoral votes? Which states strongly favored one candidate over another? Pretend you are a journalist covering the election, and write a short summary for your local paper describing the outcome of the election.

Party Politics

Words to Understand

Caucus: A meeting of members of a political party or other group.

Network: A group of people in communication, united by common interests.

Platform: A set of policy goals on which a candidate bases a campaign.

The election of George Washington was a relatively straightforward process. As the unanimous choice of the Electoral College, Washington took office with little conflict or disagreement. This cooperation in regard to the nation's leadership would not outlast the nation's first president, however. Within Washington's cabinet were two men who disagreed strongly about the ways in which the new nation should be governed. Secretary of State Thomas Jefferson favored greater power for the states, and Secretary of the Treasury Alexander Hamilton believed that America should have a strong central, or national, government. The two men differed on many other issues, including whether a bill of rights should be added to the U.S. Constitution, how debt from the Revolutionary War should be handled, and what America's position should be in foreign conflicts.

Both Jefferson and Hamilton were politically powerful men. Each had many friends who shared their views. From these differences emerged the first political parties in the United States. Supporters of Hamilton became known as Federalists, supporters of Jefferson were known as Republicans

George Washington was unanimously voted into office by the Electoral College.

(and later as Democratic-Republicans). From the election of 1800 forward, political parties would play an important role in selecting nominees for the presidency.

Jefferson's Democratic-Republican Party relied heavily on Jefferson's ideals for the U.S. government. Before the election, Jefferson wrote many letters to supporters around the country, explaining his vision and why he believed his ideas were best for America's future. Democratic-Republican supporters were encouraged to form **networks** of others who thought as they did. This ultimately formed the basis of a party structure.

The Federalist Party did not survive beyond 1816, and although it boasted the membership of the nation's first two presidents (Washington and Adams), it would never again reclaim the White House. Jefferson's Democratic-Republicans, however, would become the party we know today as the Democratic Party.

Nominating Presidents

In order to ensure that the party continued to occupy the White House when Jefferson chose to step down after two terms, Democratic-Republican leaders in Congress

The image above depicts George Washington and his cabinet, including Secretary of State Thomas Jefferson and Secretary of the Treasury Alexander Hamilton. Jefferson and Hamilton disagreed on how to run the nation. Jefferson was in favor of states having greater power, and Hamilton believed that a strong central government was best.

decided to form a committee to select the party's nominee for the presidency. This early version of a party **caucus** gave Congress the power to choose the nominees for the presidency. Supporters of various nominees would lobby hard for their favorites. The system was informal; there was no fixed time when these caucuses would meet, nor were a set number of representatives required in order to choose a nominee.

In the first three decades of presidential elections, the men who were chosen as their party's nominees shared a certain common heritage. They had all played a role in the Revolution; many had served at the Constitutional Convention. They had contacts, influence, and name recognition based on the role they had already played in shaping American government.

By 1824, political candidates no longer had the status of those who had preceded them; their names were not recognized nationally. A new generation of politicians had arisen, politicians who had become prominent because of what they had done on a local or regional level. Their support came from their individual states. A system in which individual states nominated their favorite choices proved unworkable as a system in which congressional leaders chose the nominees, however. State-based nominations would produce too many nominees, none of whom could muster enough support to win a majority of the electoral votes. A new system was needed, one that would be national but representative.

Party Conventions

The first political party to hold a convention to nominate its candidate for president was the Anti-Masonic party. This small party had no representatives in Congress, so there was no Congressional caucus that could choose the party's nominee. The party decided instead to hold a general meeting, and so, in 1831, 116 delegates from 13 states attended the party's gathering at a saloon in Baltimore. Those present selected that party's nominee for the presidency—William Wirt—and prepared a speech to outline the party's positions on the important issues of the day, a forerunner of the party **platform**.

Three months later, a second party convention was held in Baltimore—in fact, at the same saloon. There, a group of delegates opposed to President Andrew Jackson, who called themselves National Republicans (they would later become known as Whigs), also nominated a candidate, Henry Clay, and chose a platform.

The following year, the Democratic-Republicans also chose Baltimore as the location for their convention. Although Jackson, the incumbent president, was clearly the choice as nominee, Jackson wanted to hold the convention to ensure popular support for his candidacy and also to guarantee that his choice for a running mate, Martin Van

Buren, would be elected. Four years later, Jackson again championed the idea of a party convention in Baltimore, this time to guarantee the selection of his choice—Van Buren—as his successor.

These party conventions bear little resemblance to the conventions that major parties hold to nominate their presidential candidates today. In the days before television and carefully scripted speeches scheduled for prime-time coverage, the conventions were informal and often rowdy.

A CHANGING SCHEDULE

In the 1952 election, Dwight Eisenhower, the Republican candidate (who would go on to win the presidency that year), announced his candidacy on June 4, 1952—only 33 days before the Republican convention was held. Nearly 40 years later, Democrat Bill Clinton announced his candidacy on October 3, 1991, a full 284 days before the convention. Clinton's challenger in the primaries, Paul Tsongas, had declared that he would be a candidate on April 30, 1991—440 days before the Democratic convention.

The general public played only a minimal role in these conventions. Party leaders chose the delegates to the convention, decided the agenda for the conventions, and were instrumental in selecting the presidential and vice-presidential nominees. The kind of negotiation involved in determining who the nominees would be and on what issues the party would focus was largely carried on in secret, behind the scenes.

Since the 1970s, primaries and caucuses have replaced party conventions as the principal way in which presidential nominees are selected. Today, conventions provide a forum for parties to highlight their platforms and celebrate their nominees, but they rarely offer surprises. This has not always been the case. Three conventions—all held in Chicago—show how these party gatherings once directly affected the presidential election.

For the 1860 presidential election, the Republican Party held its convention in Chicago. The choice would prove fateful. It was only the second presidential convention held since the party was formed, and there were many contenders for the nomination. The location of the convention, however, provided a boost to the candidate from Illinois: Abraham Lincoln. The convention was packed with supporters from Illinois, who cheered loudly for their local candidate. At the time the convention was held, Lincoln was considered as a possible vice-presidential nominee at best, but with the loud and boisterous support of the Illinois faction, Lincoln became the presidential nominee.

Another Republican convention, in 1912, showed the influence of former presidents on the nominating process. Four years earlier, President Theodore Roosevelt had wholeheartedly supported the candidacy of his friend and former secretary of war, William Howard Taft. Roosevelt had campaigned for Taft and helped ensure that Taft would be his successor and continue Roosevelt's progressive agenda. What a difference a presidential term can make, though! Roosevelt grew dissatisfied with Taft's policies, and at the Republican convention of 1912, Roosevelt not only refused to support Taft, he actually challenged him for the nomination. When it became clear that Roosevelt would not succeed in his effort to wrestle the nomination away from Taft, Roosevelt stormed out of the convention, followed by his supporters, formed his own party—the Progressive Party—and ran as its nominee for the presidency. The split between supporters of Taft and Roosevelt divided the Republican Party and ensured that the Democratic nominee, Woodrow Wilson, would win the election.

Key moments in the history of the Republican convention.

The Democratic Party Convention of 1968, held in Chicago, has become infamous as one of the most chaotic conventions in American history. Perhaps it is not surprising that, after that election, primaries began to replace conventions as the principal path to naming the presidential nominee. Three men—Eugene McCarthy, Robert Kennedy, and Hubert Humphrey—all vied for the Democratic nomination that year. Kennedy was assassinated after winning the California primary. McCarthy represented a wing of the party opposed to the war in Vietnam. Humphrey, then vice president under Lyndon Johnson, had entered the race late, when President Johnson announced his decision not to seek re-election. He was then saddled with answering questions about the Johnson administration's war policies.

Protestors gathered outside the convention and quickly entered into violent confrontation with the Chicago police. Inside the convention hall, supporters of McCarthy and Humphrey clashed over what the party's position should be on the war in Vietnam. The violence inside and outside the Democratic Party convention helped ensure a Republican victory that year.

Protests and violent outbreaks characterized the 1968 Democratic Party Convention in Chicago, making it one of the most infamous conventions in U.S. history. In this picture, a Chicago Park District truck was used to spray tear gas to disperse crowds in Grant Park.

Primary Season

The process of choosing a party's nominee has become a increasingly function of the primary election. Through the primary and caucus, voters are given the opportunity to directly elect convention delegates who support the candidate of their choice within their party.

The primary is a product of the twentieth century. The first presidential primary election was held in Florida in 1904; by 1912, 13 states were holding primaries. In 1913, President Woodrow Wilson publicly urged the creation of a national primary system as a way for voters, rather than nominating committees or conventions, to select presidential candidates.

Real growth in the primary system did not take place until later in the twentieth century. Generally, most states hold either primaries or caucuses. A primary is much like a general election: voters go to a polling place and cast a vote for the candidate of their choice, usually within the political party to which the voter is registered. A caucus is more like a mini-convention: party members meet and

The Iowa Caucuses are electoral events where Democratic and Republican parties in the state meet to select delegates who will decide their party's nominee in the presidential election. Pictured above, 2016 presidential candidate Ted Cruz gives a speech at the Iowa Caucus.

listen to speeches in a public place before voting for delegates to represent a candidate at the national convention. In some states, only voters registered to a particular political party may vote in that party's primary. In other states, voters may vote for a candidate in another party. In all states, voters may participate in only one primary.

Presidential primaries and caucuses are usually held from February to June of an election year. Republican and Democratic primaries and caucuses are usually held on the same day. The first caucus is held in Iowa, and the first primary is held in New Hampshire. Pressure has been placed on the Democratic and Republican parties to change the schedule for primaries, however. It is argued that the schedule gives certain states—such as Iowa and New Hampshire—an unfair advantage in choosing presidential nominees. Because of the expense of a presidential campaign, candidates will often test the waters in these early primaries. If they do not receive sufficient support, they will pull out of the primaries before voters in most states have had a chance to cast their ballots.

The Role of Third Parties

Although the Republican and Democratic parties play a dominant role in presidential elections, third parties have influenced the political process throughout our history. America is often described as having a two-party political system, because presidential elections have generally focused on the candidates from two parties.

These parties have changed throughout our history. In America's earliest elections, the presidential race pitted Federalists against Anti-Federalists or Democratic-Republicans. Later, the Whigs emerged to challenge Democrats, and in the mid-1800s, the Republican Party was formed. In our recent history, presidential elections—and indeed most local and state elections, as well—have focused on Democratic and Republican candidates.

Smaller, so-called third parties have played a role in many presidential elections. These parties are usually formed when a group of people becomes alienated from the major political parties, often over a single issue. They split off and form their own party, and so throughout American history we have had candidates

In the 2016 presidential election, Dr. Jill Stein represented the Green Party.

from the Anti-Masonic Party, the Free Soil Party, the Constitutional Union Party, the Populist Party, the Progressive Party, the States' Rights Party, the American Independent Party, the Reform Party, and the Green Party (among many others) waging campaigns for the White House.

Parties that are formed around a single issue seldom succeed in winning enough nationwide support to capture the presidency. Often, as concern about that single issue fades, support for the party fades. In addition, when a third party champions a particular issue that seems to appeal to a large number of voters, that issue is often "stolen" or picked up by one or both major parties and becomes a part of their platform.

Text-Dependent Questions

1. Who was the last president from the Federalist Party?

2. What was the first political party to hold a convention to nominate its candidate for president?

3. In what state is the first presidential primary held during an election year?

Research Project

Research a third party (i.e., a party that is neither Democrat nor Republican) that is active in American politics today. Write a brief report giving an overview of the party's history; key figures in its development; its current leadership; the state, local, and national elections it has participated in, along with notable candidates; and its policy platforms. Include information about the size of its membership and the region(s) of the country where it enjoys the most support.

The Presidential Campaign

Words to Understand

Aristocratic: Relating to the ruling class of society.
Elitist: One who puts oneself above common tastes, attitudes, or fashions and believes that society should be ruled by others of a similar viewpoint.
Pragmatist: A person who favors practical strategies and solutions to problems rather than ideals.
Quagmire: A problem or situation that is difficult to solve and easily gets worse.
Telegenic: An image that works well on television.

The race for the presidency is more like a marathon than a sprint. It has not always been this way. In the earliest presidential elections, candidates announced their desire to become president in the year in which the election was held. In fact, it is only recently that candidates have begun their campaigns sometimes more than two years before an election is actually held.

The campaign season, whether short or long, has traditionally given candidates the opportunity to present themselves to voters. It also has transformed presidential elections into a kind of entertainment, in which candidates are packaged, almost like a product, to be sold to voters.

Andrew Jackson was one of the first presidential candidates to campaign. Pictured here is a poster used in his campaign.

Methought the souls of all that I had murder'd came to my tent. Act 5 Sc 3.

RICHARD III.

Candidates identify themselves with a particular image, a particular phrase or event, or even another political figure, in order to explain to the voter who they are and what they stand for. Television has further transformed presidential campaigns. Now candidates must be attractive and **telegenic**, conveying their ideas and plans in quick, colorful scenes, usually in beautiful or interesting settings, with enthusiastic crowds applauding.

Whether candidates are staged before the camera or use slogans and imagery, however, presidential campaigns have provided voters with an opportunity to better understand the individuals running for president—or at least to get a better understanding of the image the candidates wish to project.

Old Hickory and Log Cabins

In the early years of presidential elections, campaigning for the office was considered undignified. Those seeking the presidency were nominated by their peers. These people had been instrumental in shaping the country that the United States would become. Many had participated in the decision for the colonies to declare independence from Great Britain; they had served in the Revolutionary War or in the Continental Congress and later had helped to craft the Constitution that would provide the framework for the American government. They were well known to those who would vote for or against them. Their positions were clear and were illustrated by their party affiliation.

Andrew Jackson was one of the first to campaign actively for the presidency, using his image and dynamic personality to demonstrate to voters his fitness for office. The Jackson campaign in the election of 1828 marked a new era in politics—an end to the dignified pursuit of the office and a beginning of efforts to appeal directly to voters' emotions. The Jackson campaign held parades and rallies. Jackson's military career was highlighted and was used to describe him as a "new Washington" or "second Washington." He was depicted as a man of the people, a frontiersman, a man with little formal education and the nickname of "Old Hickory"—images used to contrast him with the **aristocratic** John Quincy Adams. In fact, the "Old Hickory" nickname became a focal point for the campaign: Hickory poles were put up alongside roads and in the center of towns by Jackson supporters. It was this campaign that marked the real beginning of the use of a candidate's image as part of the campaign. Voters were not supporting a party or a philosophy, but a specific man, wanting him to serve as their president.

The election of 1840 featured another military hero as candidate—General William Henry Harrison—whose supporters wisely copied many of the strategies that had brought Andrew Jackson to the White House. Harrison was the candidate for the recently formed Whig Party. He was challenging the incumbent, President Martin Van Buren, in his bid for re-election.

Harrison was presented to voters both as a military hero and as a farmer who lived on the frontier in a log cabin and was happiest drinking a cup of hard (alcoholic) cider—a drink associated with the West. Harrison was compared to George Washington when supporters spoke of his career in the military. Campaign ads focused on his generosity, suggesting that the military hero waited in his log cabin to welcome other veterans and offer them a cup of cider. The ads contrasted him with President Van Buren, who was depicted as an **elitist** snob who would be happier sipping champagne.

This image making was astonishingly effective, if glaringly inaccurate. Harrison's home, depicted as a humble log cabin on the Western frontier, was actually a 16-room mansion in Ohio. He had grown up wealthy on a Virginia plantation, the son of a signer of the Declaration of Independence, whereas the "aristocratic" President Van Buren, his opponent, had actually grown up in very humble circumstances.

The "Log Cabin and Hard Cider" campaign sparked tremendous public enthusiasm for Harrison and his running mate, John Tyler. The public eagerly supported "Tippecanoe and Tyler Too" ("Tippecanoe" was a reference to Harrison's 1811 victory against the Indians in the Battle of Tippecanoe). A weekly newspaper—the *Log Cabin*—printed stories of Harrison's heroic actions in battle, his generosity to the men who had fought with him, and his hospitality to strangers who came to visit his "cabin," as well as details of campaign rallies and the enthusiastic crowds who attended. The Whig Party organized a cabin raising, at which supporters gathered with logs brought from their farms, and built a cabin, which became the Whig party headquarters. Miniature cabins were carried in parades, and barrels of hard cider were provided at every gathering.

Listen to William Henry Harrison's campaign theme song.

In this woodcut used as an advertisement during the presidential election of 1840, General William Henry Harrison is shown in front of his log cabin, greeting a soldier and offering some hard cider. During the campaign, Harrison was depicted as a generous everyman who enjoyed drinking alcoholic cider and greeting fellow veterans.

The campaign was successful at both promoting Harrison and inspiring men (for it was only men at that time) to vote. Voter turnout was higher in that election than in any previous election; Whigs won the popular vote and captured 79 percent of the electoral vote.

The Rough Rider

Certain themes emerged from the Log Cabin campaign that would permanently alter the way candidates pursued the White House. For one, campaigns began to focus on telling a story about a candidate—one that would appeal to voters, perhaps providing him with a background that struck a chord, depicting the candidate in an idealized light or focusing on a particular element of his history or experience.

For much of the nineteenth century, many presidential candidates would be portrayed as having come from some humble background, having spent some or all of their childhood in a log cabin. Abraham Lincoln, when he ran for the presidency in 1860, was certainly one of these candidates. He was depicted as "Honest Abe," who had grown up in a log cabin on the frontier and worked splitting rails. In fact, Lincoln's image as a rail splitter became a gimmick; thousands of rails were distributed while he was campaigning, each one supposedly split by Lincoln himself.

Theodore Roosevelt's candidacy marked a new era in presidential campaigning—one in which voters chose a candidate for his personality as much as for his policies. Roosevelt had been a hero, popular for his exploits as leader of the volunteer Rough Riders during the 1898 Spanish-American War. Roosevelt became governor of New York, then was nominated for vice president on the Republican ticket with incumbent President William McKinley. McKinley had won his first term using a "front porch" campaign; instead of traveling across the country to meet with voters, the voters came to him. Formally dressed, he would emerge from his home several times a day to welcome groups of admiring visitors, all of whom had been carefully prescreened, who had scheduled their appointments well in advance, and who, before their visits, had presented McKinley's team with the issues they wanted to discuss and a copy of any remarks they intended to make.

McKinley won the office using this stately style of campaigning, so he had little incentive to leave the White House to campaign for a second term. He left that to his vice presidential nominee, and Teddy Roosevelt took to the campaign trail with vigor and enthusiasm. Roosevelt delivered fiery speeches that inspired his listeners as he crisscrossed the country, visiting 567 towns in 24 states, making 673 speeches, and spending two months campaigning in the West.

Roosevelt assumed the presidency after McKinley was assassinated while in office. He hit the campaign trail with energy and enthusiasm again in 1904 to win an additional term. Roosevelt's campaign strategy was positive, focusing on the candidate almost as a larger-than-life figure. One campaign gimmick, highlighting Roosevelt's trademark grin, was an item called "Teddy's Teeth," a whistle in the shape of Roosevelt's wide smile that could be used as a noisemaker at rallies. Another trademark survives to this day: the Teddy Bear, originally manufactured in response to a story in which President Roosevelt, on a hunting trip in 1902, was presented with a young bear to shoot. Roosevelt reportedly refused to shoot a bear that had already been captured, and stuffed bears named after him were soon being sold as political symbols.

Theodore Roosevelt changed the way people voted for president of the United States. Aside from his political policies, Roosevelt's personality, charisma, and charm played a huge role in his campaign. He toured the nation giving inspiring speeches and winning votes based on his public persona.

Roosevelt used the presidency as a stage—a "bully pulpit," in his words. He left office in 1909 but continued to capture public attention with a highly publicized big-game hunting trip he took to Africa. Dissatisfied with the policies of his Republican successor, William Howard Taft, Roosevelt determined to challenge Taft for the Republican nomination in 1912; when Taft won the nomination, Roosevelt formed his own party and ran for the presidency as the Progressive Party candidate.

Changing Techniques

The technological changes of the 20th century dramatically impacted how candidates campaigned for the presidency. Changes in transportation—the development of railroads, automobiles, and airplanes—made it easy for candidates to travel across the country to present their programs directly to the voters. Changes in communication—the development of film, radio, telephones, television, and the Internet—have all influenced the ways in which candidates are presented and how presidential campaigns are conducted.

At one time, campaigns relied on political rallies, friendly newspaper coverage, songs, buttons, and tokens to promote their candidates to the public. In 1920, the right to vote was extended to women with the Nineteenth Amendment to the Constitution. It was not until 1952, however, that women made up half of the country's voters, and campaigns increasingly focused on efforts to design ads that appealed to women. Some of these seem amusingly outdated, such as the potholder featuring Republican candidate Dwight Eisenhower's face, or the stockings embroidered with the phrase "I like Ike" (Eisenhower's nickname). Campaigns also began to feature not only the candidate but also his wife and family. The candidates' wives hit the campaign trail, often separately from their husbands.

By the 1950s, television advertising had become a critical element for presidential campaigns. The first political advertising occurred in 1952, when 20-second commercials for Eisenhower were aired during popular television programs such as *I Love Lucy*. This strategy proved so successful at reaching large numbers of potential voters that it has continued to this day.

Certain commercials have been particularly noteworthy in presidential campaigns. In 1964, for instance, a television ad (the "Daisy Girl" ad) made for the re-election campaign of President Lyndon Johnson showed a little girl

In this 1976 photograph, Democratic candidate Jimmy Carter stands on his peanut farm in Plains, Georgia. Jimmy Carter emphasized his background as a peanut farmer far more than his experience as governor of Georgia to appeal to the American public.

plucking the petals off a flower, replaced by images of a nuclear explosion, implying that if Johnson's opponent, Republican Barry Goldwater, were to be elected, he might start a nuclear war. In 1976, commercials featuring Democratic candidate Jimmy Carter nearly always depicted him dressed casually, usually in a rural setting, emphasizing his background as a Georgia peanut farmer and his status as a Washington outsider.

In 1984, television commercials for President Ronald Reagan's re-election campaign told voters, "It's morning again in America," and reminded them that the country was "prouder and stronger and better" than it had been fewer than "four short years ago." In 2000, when domestic issues were the focus of the presidential campaign, one fascinating ad from then-Governor George W. Bush warned voters a year before the September 11 attacks, "We live in a dangerous world of terror, madmen, and missiles." At a time when few Americans were focusing on the threat of terrorist attacks, it is interesting that the candidate promised to "rebuild our military" and promote a "foreign policy with a touch of iron." Four years later, political commercials for both President Bush and his Democratic challenger, Senator John Kerry, focused on the ideas of "changing times" and the need for a "safe America."

Twenty-First-Century Campaigns

The 2008 presidential campaign season began nearly two years before Election Day, when Democrat Barack Obama and Republican John McCain, both U.S. senators, announced their candidacies in February 2007. Once both men had secured their respective parties' nomination in late summer of 2008, the official campaign was underway. Obama's campaign focused on his youth, vitality, and ability to be an agent of change. His campaign slogan, "Change We Can Believe In," stated this explicitly. He appealed to voters who wanted to move away from the policies of the Bush era, particularly the **quagmire** of the Iraq War. McCain presented himself as a maverick who spurned political orthodoxies and was able to work with both parties to get things done. The official slogan "Country First" nodded to his patriotic views: McCain was a former prisoner of war in Vietnam, and his battle-tested persona was born out of lived experience.

Obama won a second term in 2012 after defeating Republican challenger Mitt Romney. This set the stage for a contentious 2016 campaign that would draft new Democratic and Republican candidates. When the dust settled after drawn-out primaries on both sides, Democrat Hillary Clinton and Republican Donald Trump faced each other in the general election.

Clinton emphasized her experience as a former first lady, U.S. senator from New York, and secretary of state under President Obama. She cast herself as a **pragmatist** who understood how the world worked, yet was open to progressive ideas such as women's and LGBT rights. The slogan "Stronger Together" tried to encapsulate her inclusive message. Trump was a former real estate developer and reality television star who used his name recognition and celebrity to appeal to

U.S. Senator Barack Obama gives a speech at a "Change We Need" presidential rally in North Carolina in 2008.

voters. His signature phrase "Make America Great Again" became both a campaign slogan and a cultural phenomenon. Red baseball caps emblazoned with the message were ubiquitous at pro-Trump rallies across the country. The fact that he had no previous political experience was seen as an advantage by many voters who, for years, had felt left behind by the Washington elite.

Text-Dependent Questions

1. What presidential candidate was known as "Old Hickory?"

2. How did William McKinley's campaign differ from traditional campaigns?

3. Which president was the first to use television advertising for his campaign?

Research Project

Select a twenty-first century presidential race. Using the Internet, research archived videos of campaign advertisements for the two candidates. Write a brief report summarizing the content and tone of these advertisements, including information about how they differed, how they were the same, and the ways in which each candidate presented him- or herself, his or her platform, and his or her opponent.

6

Promoting the Message

Words to Understand

Canvassing: Going door-to-door to raise awareness about a particular candidate or political issue.

Data mining: The process of analyzing large amounts of information in order to draw conclusions or discover patterns.

Demographic: A specific category of a population.

Political action committee: An organization that raises funds to influence elections, ballot measures, or other legislation.

Pollster: A person who conducts a survey, or poll, to determine voter preferences.

Modern presidential candidates generally have on their staffs multiple people responsible for the various stages of a campaign. Among these is usually at least one media consultant, who provides advice and expertise on the kinds of commercials to create, the issues on which to focus, and the image of the candidate that should be presented. Media consultants are well informed on issues that appeal to voters who watch certain television programs, and they will place specific commercials focusing on those issues during those programs. If you become familiar with a particular candidate's political advertising, you will notice that a different

Kellyanne Conway served as one of Donald Trump's campaign advisers in the 2016 presidential election. She was the first woman to run a successful presidential campaign.

commercial will appear during a news program, a sports event, or a morning talk show. Each of these ads might focus on a different issue or present the candidate in a different way.

Television campaign ads use certain basic strategies to prompt a response in viewers. Ads attacking an opponent frequently show that person in black and white, perhaps with footage played at a slower speed, or shot from an unflattering angle. Ads promoting a candidate frequently position the camera slightly below the candidate to make him or her seem taller and more regal, so that the viewer literally looks up to the candidate. Depending on what image the ad wishes to convey, the candidate may be shown speaking before a cheering crowd with American flags in the background, with rolled-up sleeves and chatting informally with a group of workers, in a classroom with young children, or relaxed at home, surrounded by loving family members.

Music is also an important element of political commercials; it may be ominous or somber in an ad criticizing an opponent, or patriotic and uplifting when promoting a candidate. The central issue of the commercial is generally condensed into a few key phrases, something like: "Candidate X: Can You Really Trust Him?" or "Candidate Y: Working for a Bright Future."

Television commercials can be the most expensive part of a presidential campaign. For this reason, candidates will also use televised campaign events—covered for free by the media—as an opportunity to promote their message and appeal to a specific group of voters.

Social Media

Today's campaigns go well beyond the television and radio spots of the past. The connectivity of the Internet and social media sites like Facebook, Twitter, and Instagram mean that candidates have new avenues to reach voters. Hillary Clinton supporters—including celebrities like Katy Perry—got the hashtag #ImWithHer trending during the 2016 election so much that it became another campaign slogan. New phone-banking software allows people to make calls on behalf of a candidate from their laptop; the software dials, connects, and stores information about the call, allowing candidates to reach a vast amount of people in a quick and efficient way.

More and more campaign contributions are now made online through fundraising sites like ActBlue. These sites save donors' contact information and build up a valuable database of email addresses that can be used by future candidates. Both

Katy Perry was one of many celebrities who came forward in 2016 to support Democratic candidate Hillary Clinton. Pictured here, Perry stands with Clinton and other supporters at a campaign rally.

Clinton and Trump used text messaging to communicate directly with supporters. Supporters can also use social media to organize meet-ups, door-to-door canvassing, and other activities on behalf of a candidate. All of this adds up to more organized, effective political networks and more personalized campaign strategies.

Through the candidates' Web sites, social media accounts, and interactive text messaging, voters have an opportunity not simply to learn more about the candidate but also to communicate with other supporters, read blogs from the candidate and campaign staff, send messages to the candidate, or contribute to the campaign. In the 2016 Democratic primary, candidate Bernie Sanders made historical use of social media's ability to connect people and "crowdfund" a campaign. Rather than relying on large donors, Sanders fueled his presidential run through small contributions (the average was $27), many of which were made through online platforms. The campaign raised $218 million online, with over 40 percent of contributions coming from mobile phones.

NEW WAYS OF CAMPAIGNING

As part of their campaign for the 2016 presidential election, candidates explored new ways to communicate their message to voters, particularly younger ones. Taking advantage of social media sites like Twitter, Facebook, Instagram, and YouTube, presidential candidates were tweeting, posting photos, and streaming video, all in an effort to get their ideas—and faces—into the public square.

Actress Lena Dunham took over Democratic candidate Hilary Clinton's Instagram account for a day, posting images with the hashtag #ImWithHer in honor of Clinton's campaign slogan. Clinton also turned up for an appearance on comedian Zack Galifianakis's satirical talk show *Between Two Ferns*, just as president Barack Obama had in 2014 as a way to introduce the Affordable Care Act to young people. Donald Trump became famous—or infamous—for his prolific use of his Twitter account, bypassing traditional media outlets to fire his diatribes directly at his audience.

Dialed In

In order to win an election, candidates have two basic challenges: to develop a message that appeals to voters, and to deliver that message effectively. Modern polling techniques enable candidates to learn which issues matter to voters so they can target those issues with appearances and commercials. These issues can vary state by state or even from one town or city to another, which is why presidential candidates may focus on issues like gun control when speaking to one group of voters, and stem cell research when speaking to another.

Polling is the process of speaking with voters to gauge their support for candidates, policy measures, and other issues. One of the most common polling methods is the telephone survey. Polling firms such as Gallup use random-digit dialing methods to contact a cross section of voters. Here, an area code and three-digit exchange are selected, and then dialing software fills in the last four digits of the number at random. There are methods to ensure that both landline and cell phone numbers are included, though federal regulations state that auto-generated cell phone numbers must be dialed by hand. The advantage of random-digit dialing is that it connects with people whose numbers are not listed in the phone book. However, many of the

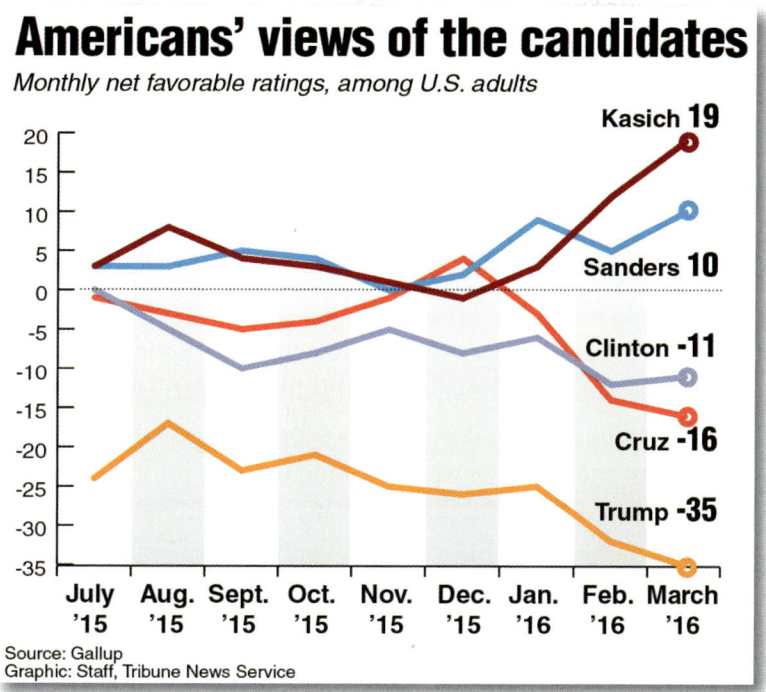

This Gallup poll shows the favorable ratings of the presidential candidates in 2016.

randomly generated numbers might not be individuals at all but businesses or other non-assigned numbers.

One major problem with telephone surveys, especially since the advent of cell phones and caller ID technology, is a low response rate. People are not as likely to answer numbers they do not recognize, and they may feel little incentive to return a **pollster's** message. It may take a pollster multiple attempts to complete a call. Whereas 20 years ago it took between 2,000 and 2,500 calls to generate a sample of 800 responders, today it takes over three times that amount. Pollsters have even offered monetary rewards to people willing to complete a survey.

Responders to a poll can share certain traits that skew the overall poll results. This is called a "non-response bias." For instance, a person who works two jobs might not have the time to answer a telephone survey, while a retiree may actually enjoy the chance to express his or her views. If more of one particular group responds to a poll than another, the poll ends up being a representation of that group's views rather than the intended cross section of society. Pollsters may give additional "weight" to the responses of certain people to better reflect the overall population.

Data Breach

In the age of the Internet, pollsters have many more options for gathering information on potential voters. There are now online polls, which are cheaper to conduct because they do not require as large a staff as telephone surveys. However, because not everyone in America has access to the Internet, online polls can only reach a limited amount of voters.

Data mining is the process of analyzing large amounts of information, such as the purchasing habits of a given group, in order to draw conclusions, make predictions, or find patterns in behavior. Almost everything we do is being tracked online: the Web sites we visit, the images we choose to share on Instagram, or the purchases we make from an online retailer. If we swipe a supermarket club card, the store might capture what we buy and the time we buy it, and use that information to make business decisions.

This sort of large-scale information analysis has impacted political polling and messaging strategies. Candidates now gather data on individual voters that they can then use to target advertising, determine potential "swing" voters, and reach new supporters through their backers' social media networks. Instead of looking at broad **demographic** groups such as senior citizens, candidates can "micro-target" messages to specific individuals. Based on a voter's data profile, for instance, a candidate may be able to tell that the voter cares strongly about environmental issues. An online advertisement about a candidate's position on global warming could then be identified as the best way to connect with this particular voter.

In 2018, the data mining firm Cambridge Analytica came under fire—and was later forced to cease operations in the United States—after news broke that it had obtained the data of up to 87 million Facebook users through dubious means. A third party had designed a Facebook app called "This Is My Digital Life." Users who downloaded the app were told that any data they supplied would be for academic research. This turned out to be false: Against Facebook's official policy, the designer of the app sold the harvested data to Cambridge Analytica, who then used it to build profiles of voters. The app also collected data on the users' Facebook friends without their knowledge or consent. The Cambridge Analytica scandal has sparked debate over the use of data mining, micro-targeting, and psychological profiling in campaigns, especially as related to privacy concerns and the ways digital media may undermine democracy.

In 2018, Cambridge Analytica was forced to cease operations in the U.S. Facebook executives were also required to testify in front of Congress about their involvement with the company and its data mining.

The Campaign Industry

In October 2018, it was reported that President Donald Trump had already raised $100 million for his re-election campaign—with the election *two full years* away. Wealthy donors were able to give large amounts across a variety of fund-raising accounts. Smaller donations of under $200 apiece also drove up the total amount in Trump's "war chest."

Money has always influenced presidential elections—after all, advertising, **canvassing** efforts, rallies, and other tools to promote a candidate are not free. Yet, there is no doubt that the cost of presidential elections has risen drastically over the past several decades. In 1960, for instance, Democratic candidate John F. Kennedy and Republican candidate Richard Nixon each spent about $10 million on their respective campaigns. Fast-forward to the 2008 election, where Democrat Barack Obama spent $760.4 million, and Republican John McCain $239.7 million, for a combined total of over $1 billion.

Clearly, political campaigns have become a huge industry. The overall cost of the 2016 presidential election, including primaries, was a whopping $2.4 billion. That number jumps to $6.5 billion when congressional elections are figured in. Increases in population and individual income have contributed to greater campaign donations and higher spending overall, but changes in political donation guidelines, the growth of **political action committees** ("PACs"), and the influence of big-money donors have all been factors as well.

The 2010 U.S. Supreme Court ruling *Citizens United v. FEC* was a landmark case for the rules of campaign finance. Previously, there were restrictions on how money from corporations, unions, and other organizations could be used to influence elections. *Citizens* removed some of these restrictions and made it possible for groups to donate unlimited amounts to "super PACs": political action committees that may not endorse individual candidates or coordinate with specific campaigns, but may strongly push a particular legislative agenda through advertising and other media outlets. Critics of *Citizens* say that it has enabled special-interest groups to dictate policy, as candidates may feel beholden to the agendas of the super PACs that support their campaigns. Other political analysts claim that the influence of *Citizens*

Donald Trump speaks at a gala hosted by the Republican Party.

is overstated, pointing to the fact that laws allowing for corporate money in politics were already in place before the decision.

How campaign finance works.

One solution to the thorny problem of campaign finance may be increased citizen participation in the fund-raising process. Recent elections have seen an increase in smaller campaign contributions spread across a larger amount of donors. The city of Seattle has experimented with a "democracy voucher" program that awards residents $100 to donate to candidates of their choosing in municipal elections. A program like this could be scaled up to the national level as a way to move toward a more democratic campaign finance system.

Text-Dependent Questions

1. What was the average donation to Bernie Sanders's campaign during the 2016 Democratic primary?
2. What is data mining?
3. Are super PACs tied to individual candidates?

Research Project

Select a Democratic or Republican candidate from one of the past three presidential elections. Research his or her campaign strategies, including social media and apps, targeted advertising (both on television and online), and campaign finance tools such as super PACs or individual donations. Write a brief overview of the campaign, including elements that were effective and those that were not. Did high spending translate to a victory for the candidate? What might this say about campaign finance?

Promoting the Message

The Presidential Candidate

Words to Understand

Enclave: A place with a distinct population or cultural character.
Misogynistic: Showing a derogatory attitude toward women.
Relief agency: An organization that facilitates assistance to people or countries in need.

If someone were to craft a want ad for a modern presidential candidate, it might look something like this:

> Wanted: Attractive, energetic, enthusiastic candidate for president of the United States. Must be willing to commit up to two years to campaign. Must be willing to travel extensively, smile continually, and chat comfortably with workers, corporate executives, small children, senior citizens, and men and women of different ages and ethnic groups, generally in the same day. Must develop a message that appeals to all Americans and deliver it, without mistake, every day. Must be willing to greet supporters and handle hecklers. Must never appear flustered, uncomfortable, confused, or tired. Must speak confidently of your qualifications to lead an entire nation. Must inspire others to share

Before you head for the polls, be sure to read about the candidates and what they stand for. Think about what you would like to see in a candidate.

your vision for America. Must be a good fundraiser and an excellent public speaker. Must be neither too slick nor too unpolished. Must have some political experience yet not be a political insider. Must understand Washington politics and yet be willing to criticize them. Must be in excellent health. Must have a past free of any trouble or scandal, and must have a loving and supportive family. Must be at least 35 years of age, and must be a natural-born citizen of the United States.

When voters are asked about their ideal presidential candidate, they often mention things like honesty, energy, moral character, ability to be calm under pressure, experience, and ideas for addressing the nation's problems. Some might stress that a candidate should be younger than a certain age, perhaps younger than 60 or 65. Others might suggest that the ideal presidential candidate would be a certain gender, or of a certain racial, religious, or ethnic background. Still others might want a presidential candidate who had served in the military, or one who enjoys hunting and spending time in the outdoors.

Few modern voters, however, would say that their ideal presidential candidate must have been born in a log cabin or must be willing to drink hard cider. Modern voters might be more inclined to vote against, rather than for, a candidate depicted as Napoleon, but in the nineteenth century, that very comparison was put to good use for Andrew Jackson. Voters no longer require a presidential candidate to be someone of humble origin, whose life demonstrates a rags-to-riches story. It would not be possible for a presidential candidate to refuse to leave his home and to conduct a campaign by inviting prescreened groups to his front porch. Voters have proven their willingness to elect presidents who were Catholic or who were divorced; both situations might have served as serious liabilities in an earlier age.

Political scientist James David Barber has suggested that there are cycles, or themes, for each presidential election, and that the successful candidate is the one who best responds to the perceived demands of voters in a particular election cycle. For instance, in one presidential election, voters might be looking for a candidate who is aggressive, a fighter willing to demonstrate his or her toughness in challenging opponents and proposing sweeping plans to lead the country. Four years later, voters might prefer a candidate who inspires them, one whose morals and conscience focus on America as a land where people help each other and do good in the world. In yet another four years, voters might elect a candidate who is a unifier, a person who promises to heal divisions within the country.

Common Trends

Although the qualifications that cause a presidential candidate to appeal to voters have changed over the years, there are certain common elements that paint a picture of the successful presidential candidate. First is education. More than two-thirds of all of the men who have been elected president have held college degrees. Nine presidents never attended college, although the majority of them were elected in the eighteenth and nineteenth centuries: George Washington, Andrew Jackson, Martin Van Buren, Zachary Taylor, Millard Fillmore, Abraham Lincoln, Andrew Johnson, Grover Cleveland, and Harry Truman. Of those who did attend college, many attended either Harvard University or Yale University. Harvard counts seven presidents as alumni: John Adams, John Quincy Adams, Teddy Roosevelt, Franklin Roosevelt, John F. Kennedy, George W. Bush (who attended Harvard Business School), and Barack Obama (who attended Harvard Law School). Five presidents have attended Yale: William Howard Taft, Gerald Ford (who attended Yale Law School), George H.W. Bush, Bill Clinton (who attended Yale Law School), and George W. Bush.

Most successful presidential candidates have demonstrated through previous political positions that they have the skills and experience necessary to lead the nation.

MOST LIKELY TO SUCCEED

The candidate who is most likely to become president of the United States, based on the average of all presidents, will have the following traits:

- ★ Is a college graduate; probably attended Harvard or Yale
- ★ Has been the governor of a state
- ★ Has a law degree
- ★ Has served in the military
- ★ Is from a small town
- ★ Is 54 years old
- ★ Is married with children

President Lincoln is one of nine presidents who never attended college. Here, he is pictured with his son William Wallace Lincoln in the early 1860s.

Fourteen men who were elected president had first served as vice presidents: John Adams, Thomas Jefferson, Martin Van Buren, John Tyler, Millard Fillmore, Andrew Johnson, Chester Arthur, Teddy Roosevelt, Calvin Coolidge, Harry Truman, Richard Nixon, Lyndon Johnson, Gerald Ford, and George H.W. Bush. Others have served as cabinet officers, ambassadors, or members of the House of Representatives or Senate.

Serving as the governor of a state is another way in which presidential candidates demonstrate their skills at executive leadership. A total of 19 presidents have served as governors of states or territories, and six (Hayes, Cleveland, Wilson, F. Roosevelt, Clinton, and G.W. Bush) were governor when they became president. Although serving as the mayor of a large city might seems like a stepping stone to the presidency, only one mayor—Grover Cleveland, mayor of Buffalo, New York—has ever become president.

Training in the law is another common trend among many of the men who have been elected president: More than two-thirds of all presidents have had some law-related education or training.

After his presidency, William Howard Taft (center) put his law education to work and was appointed as the chief justice of the United States. He is the only president to have served the country in both positions.

There are, of course, exceptions to these trends. Military service is a common trend in the background of many presidents, and three men who had no political experience were elected purely because of their service as army generals—Zachary Taylor, Ulysses S. Grant, and Dwight D. Eisenhower. Herbert Hoover never had run for any elected office before becoming president, although he had served as secretary of commerce and in several national and international **relief agencies** during World War I.

Presidents often need to be educators, and 10 presidents actually served as elementary- or secondary-school teachers: John Adams, Jackson, Fillmore, Pierce, Garfield, Arthur, Cleveland, McKinley, Harding, and Lyndon B. Johnson. Seven presidents taught at colleges or graduate schools—John Quincy Adams, Garfield, Taft, Wilson, Clinton, and Obama.

Presidential candidates once were expected to own some kind of farm or plantation, in keeping with the tradition of George Washington as the gentleman farmer. In recent years, however, only one candidate—Jimmy Carter, in 1976—has highlighted his experience working on the family farm as a critical part of his campaign.

No doctors or ministers have been elected to the presidency, although William Henry Harrison briefly studied medicine, and both John Adams and James Madison studied religion.

Most presidents have come from small towns or rural areas. Only five were born in large cities, and several (including Jackson, Polk, Fillmore, Buchanan, Lincoln, and Garfield) spent their childhoods living in log cabins.

Age is also a critical factor for many voters when they determine which candidate will receive their vote. Presidents are generally in their mid-50s when elected to the presidency. Ronald Reagan was the oldest, elected to his first term only a few weeks before his 70th birthday. John F. Kennedy was the youngest to be elected president, at age 43, although Theodore Roosevelt was the youngest man to *become* president. He was 42 years old when he succeeded William McKinley, who had been assassinated.

Many men and women choose to enter public service because a family member has held elected office, so it is not a surprise that several presidents are related to others who have been elected president. John Quincy Adams was the son of President John Adams, and President George H.W. Bush's son, George W. Bush, also was elected president. James Madison and Zachary Taylor were second cousins, and

William Henry Harrison was the grandfather of Benjamin Harrison. Fifth cousins Theodore Roosevelt and Franklin Roosevelt both became president.

A look at Roosevelt family relations.

Most presidents have been married, although not all were married at the time of their election. James Buchanan is the only president who never married. Cleveland, Tyler, and Wilson all married during their presidencies.

The majority of presidents have had children, either their own or stepchildren or adopted children. Tyler, with 15, holds the honor of having had the most children.

Being born in the eastern part of the country seems to offer an advantage to presidential candidates, although this has not necessarily been true in recent elections. The state that has produced the most successful presidential candidates is Virginia, with eight: Washington, Jefferson, Madison, Monroe, William Henry Harrison, Tyler, Taylor, and Wilson.

What the Experts Say

Although these broad characteristics shape a general picture of the background of the successful presidential candidate, there are certain other elements, particularly in modern elections, that can determine how and why a president is elected.

Matthew Dowd, director of polling and media planning for George W. Bush during his 2000 presidential campaign, notes three key events that helped Bush win the primaries and ultimately go on to win the presidency. First, the Bush campaign focused intensely on raising large sums of money early in the campaign. Second, it gained many endorsements from important and popular Republican figures. Third, the campaign was able to successfully "spin" (or influence) press coverage to position Bush as the front-runner for the Republican nomination, according to Kathleen Hall Jamieson and Paul Waldman in *Electing the President 2000: The Insiders' View*.

"Change" became the key theme of the 2008 campaign, both in the primaries and the general election. The financial crisis of 2008 and the ongoing Iraq War were the main issues that motivated voters. In 2013, Jesse Holcomb of the Pew Research Center pointed to Republican candidate John McCain's claim that "the fundamentals of our economy are strong" even as financial markets were unraveling worldwide as an example of an "apparent tactical misstep" that may have contributed to his loss. In a 2013 piece for the *Guardian*, political analyst Harry J. Enten cited sitting president George W. Bush's dismal approval ratings as another factor that worked against McCain.

According to *Shattered: Inside Hillary Clinton's Doomed 2016 Campaign* by journalists Jon Allen and Amie Parnes, Clinton's loss to Donald Trump in the 2016 general election was brought about by a mismanaged staff, a failure to visit important working-class **enclaves** in the Rust Belt and the Midwest, and a set of policy proposals that never truly jelled. The day after the election, writer and policy maker Robert L. Borosage published a piece entitled "Why Trump Won" in the *Nation*. Trump "promised change to a country desperate for it," Borosage wrote, and this desperation—stemming from economic inequality and frustration with politics as

The 42nd president of the United States, Bill Clinton, served two terms in office, from 1993 to 2001. One key to his presidential win was his campaign's focus on the economy, health care, and the need for change.

usual—made people willing to overlook Trump's history of racist, **misogynistic**, and anti-immigrant remarks. Other studies have not been as forgiving of the electorate, however, and have shown that racial resentment may have played a part in Trump's victory. Correspondent German Lopez examined some of these distressing findings in a 2017 article for the Web site Vox.

How a President Is Elected

Every four years, Americans are given the opportunity to select a new candidate to become their president. Although those elected to the highest office in the land have so far all been men, it seems likely that the presidency will become more diverse, both in terms of gender and race, in the future.

The delegates to the Constitutional Convention who gathered in Philadelphia in 1787 carefully considered the process by which a president would be elected. They formulated the plan for an electoral college—a group of educated, wealthy, and prominent men who would carefully study and debate the qualifications of the various candidates before deciding which man would make the best president. The creation of political parties, the increase of public participation in an election, and the arrival of conventions, campaigns, and public scrutiny of candidates have dramatically transformed what was intended to be a careful, deliberative process into a media circus.

Although the Electoral College was initially intended to address the concerns of smaller states—that their voices might not carry weight in presidential elections—the reality is that certain, more heavily populated states are considered key to elections and receive intense focus during presidential campaigns. The states with the largest numbers of electoral votes—California, Texas, New York, Florida, Illinois, Pennsylvania, and Ohio—receive a significant portion of a candidate's attention and campaign resources.

Political parties—an insignificant factor in the election of the nation's first president—quickly became a key element in how a candidate for the presidency is selected and, ultimately, elected. Party conventions, although no longer the critical factor in selecting the nominee for the presidency, still provide a framework for a candidate to rally support and present the official platform for the campaign.

The extensive campaign season also plays a key role in how a president is elected. Candidates must develop a message that appeals to voters and then present that message effectively. They must raise large amounts of money to sustain the

U.S. president George W. Bush (right) and his challenger, Democratic candidate John Kerry (left), engage in their first presidential debate on September 30, 2004. Both candidates had qualities that would appeal to voters, including specific policy plans and prior political experience.

expenses of a campaign, must gain the support of prominent and popular people, and must use the media effectively—through advertisements, interviews, and other appearances—to convince as many voters as possible that they are the best qualified to serve as the next president of the United States.

The election of a president remains one of the most important events in American politics, providing every eligible citizen with the opportunity to choose the person they want to lead the country. George Washington was the unanimous choice to be the nation's first president, but from that smooth and unified beginning has come a process that is more often marked by division and disagreement. People become deeply involved in the process of choosing a president, and strong emotions may mark the search for the best-qualified candidate. Candidates face hazards, obstacles, and unanticipated events that may turn their road to the White House into a dead end. They need skill, endurance, and luck if they are to transition from candidate to president.

The process of choosing a president has changed in many ways from that first presidential election in 1789. The hope is that each change will make the process more democratic, ensuring that all Americans have a voice in choosing the person who will become their president.

Text-Dependent Questions

1. Name three presidents who never attended college.

2. Has a mayor of an American city ever become president? If so, who?

3. According to Stanley Greenberg, what was one reason for Al Gore's defeat in 2000?

Research Project

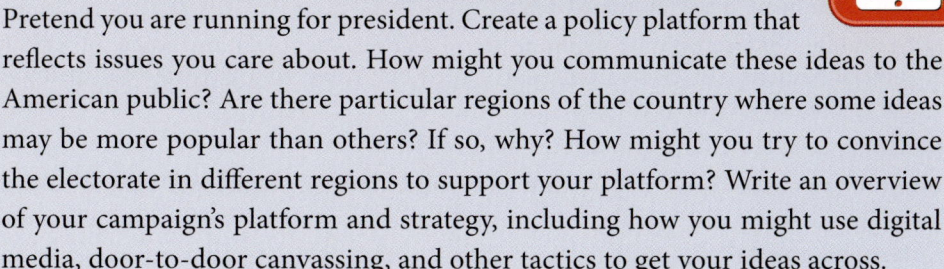

Pretend you are running for president. Create a policy platform that reflects issues you care about. How might you communicate these ideas to the American public? Are there particular regions of the country where some ideas may be more popular than others? If so, why? How might you try to convince the electorate in different regions to support your platform? Write an overview of your campaign's platform and strategy, including how you might use digital media, door-to-door canvassing, and other tactics to get your ideas across.

Series Glossary of Key Terms

Abolitionist: A person committed to abolishing a certain practice, such as slavery or unfair criminal justice practices.

Acquittal: When a person is cleared of a charge of an offense.

Ambassador: A person who acts as the representative of a nation, organization, or other group in discussions or negotiations with others.

Amnesty: To give an official pardon to a person accused of an offense.

Appeal: In legal terms, to apply to a higher court to review, and possibly overturn, the decision of a lower court.

Apportionment: The division of something, such as money, among a group.

Bicameral: Used to describe a legislative body with two chambers.

Bond: A type of financial instrument in which the issuer agrees to repay an investor a certain amount of money with interest over time.

Cabinet: In government, a group of advisers of a head of state.

Canvass: To appeal directly to people in hopes of securing their votes.

Casework: Assistance in matters of government provided by a senator to a constituent, including answering questions, explaining policies, or determining eligibility.

Caucus: A gathering of members of a specific political party or organization to form policy positions, choose leaders, and make other decisions relevant to the organization.

Censure: To formally and publicly express disapproval of a person or action.

Census: An official count of a population, often including other data or information about that population.

Centrist: A politician who favors policies that are neither too liberal nor too conservative.

Chief justice: The highest ranking judge on a court with multiple judges; in the United States, the head of the Supreme Court.

Civil service: The professional public sector of a government (not including the military, judicial branches, or elected officials), staffed by people who are hired for their skills rather than elected or appointed.

Cloture: A means of ending debate on a bill in order to force a vote.

Common law: Laws based on past custom, or what has been judged over time to be lawful or unlawful.

Conference committee: In the U.S. Congress, a temporary committee made up of both House and Senate members, organized to prepare a version of an act that incorporates amendments from both chambers.

Constituent: A person who can vote and is represented by a public official.

Decentralized: Used to describe a system in which power is dispersed among people, states, or other entities, rather than controlled by one administrative body.

Deficit spending: When a government spends money that it has borrowed rather than collected through taxes.
Delegate: A person dispatched to represent others at a conference, legislative session, or other official event.
Demographic: A specific part of a population.
Deposition: Testimony taken down in writing.
Diplomat: An official representative of one country to another.
Duty: A tax or fee placed on imported or exported goods.
Egalitarian: Of or related to the belief that humans are equal, especially with respect to social, political, and economic rights and privileges.
Electoral College: A body of representatives from each state, who formally vote to elect the president and vice president.
Excise tax: A tax on a specific good or activity, often included in the overall price.
Executive branch: The U.S. government entity that enforces laws, with the president at its head.
Extrajudicial: Describing an act that is not legally authorized.
Federal deficit: The amount of money the federal government spends in excess of what it collects in taxes.
Federalist: An advocate of a central national government that unites states and leaves various powers to state governments.
Filibuster: The strategy of legislators talking indefinitely to prevent a vote on a bill.
Franchise: An individual's right to vote.
Gold standard: A monetary system where the value of currency is based on a specific quantity of gold.
Habeas corpus: A legal means by which a person can contest unlawful imprisonment; the term is Latin for "You have the body."
Impeachment: A charge of wrongdoing or misconduct against a public official that may result in termination from office.
Inaugurate: To begin a policy or practice; to formally admit someone into a public office.
Incumbent: A person currently holding a political office.
Indict: To formally charge someone of a crime.
Isolationist: A policy that favors limited or no engagement in international affairs.
Legislature: The assembly of a government or state that is tasked with making laws.
Libertarian: A person who believes completely in the free will and choice of individuals.
Line-item veto: The power of a chief executive to reject certain parts of a bill.
Lobbyist: A person who advocates for particular policies or positions.
Mandate: An instruction to do something in a certain way.
Motion: A formal proposal or request put before a legislative body.

Naturalization: The process of granting a person from one country citizenship of another country.

Originalism: When referring to the U.S. Constitution, a belief that the document should be interpreted along the lines of the Framers' original intent.

Pardon: To release someone of all punishments for a crime.

Parliamentarian: A person who advises a legislative body on matters of procedure.

Partisanship: Strong adherence to a particular cause or group, often at the expense of compromise with others.

Perjury: An act of lying under oath.

Platform: A set of policy goals on which a candidate bases a campaign.

Pocket veto: When a president indirectly vetoes a bill by leaving it unsigned as a legislative session expires.

Political action committee: An organization that raises funds to influence elections, ballot measures, or other legislation.

Polling: In politics, soliciting the opinions of the public to help determine electoral preferences.

Primary: An election within a political party to choose its candidates for a race.

Progressive: In political science, a person who seeks to advance society through implementation of new policies and ideas.

Pro tempore: A Latin phrase meaning "for the time being," used to describe when a person holds a position in the absence of a superior.

Provision: A requirement, restriction, or condition set forth in a legal document.

Quorum: The minimum number of members of a group who need to be present in order to officially conduct business.

Recession: A period of economic decline, with drops in both trade and production of goods.

Reprieve: To grant a delay in sentencing for a crime.

Resolution: A formal proposal adopted by a governing body.

Secession: The formal withdrawal from a state, alliance, or other political body.

Slip law: A document containing the complete text of a new law along with its legislative history, often the law's first published form.

Subpoena: A formal document ordering someone to provide evidence or testimony, most often to a court.

Subsidized: Funded by an outside source.

Suffragist: A person who advocates for others' right to vote.

Supermajority: A vote total that represents significantly more than one-half of the voting assembly, often 60 percent or two-thirds.

Tariff: A tax on imported or exported goods.

Treason: An act of betraying one's country.

Veto: The power to reject a legislative bill and refuse to sign it into law.